Pokémon Sun & Moon

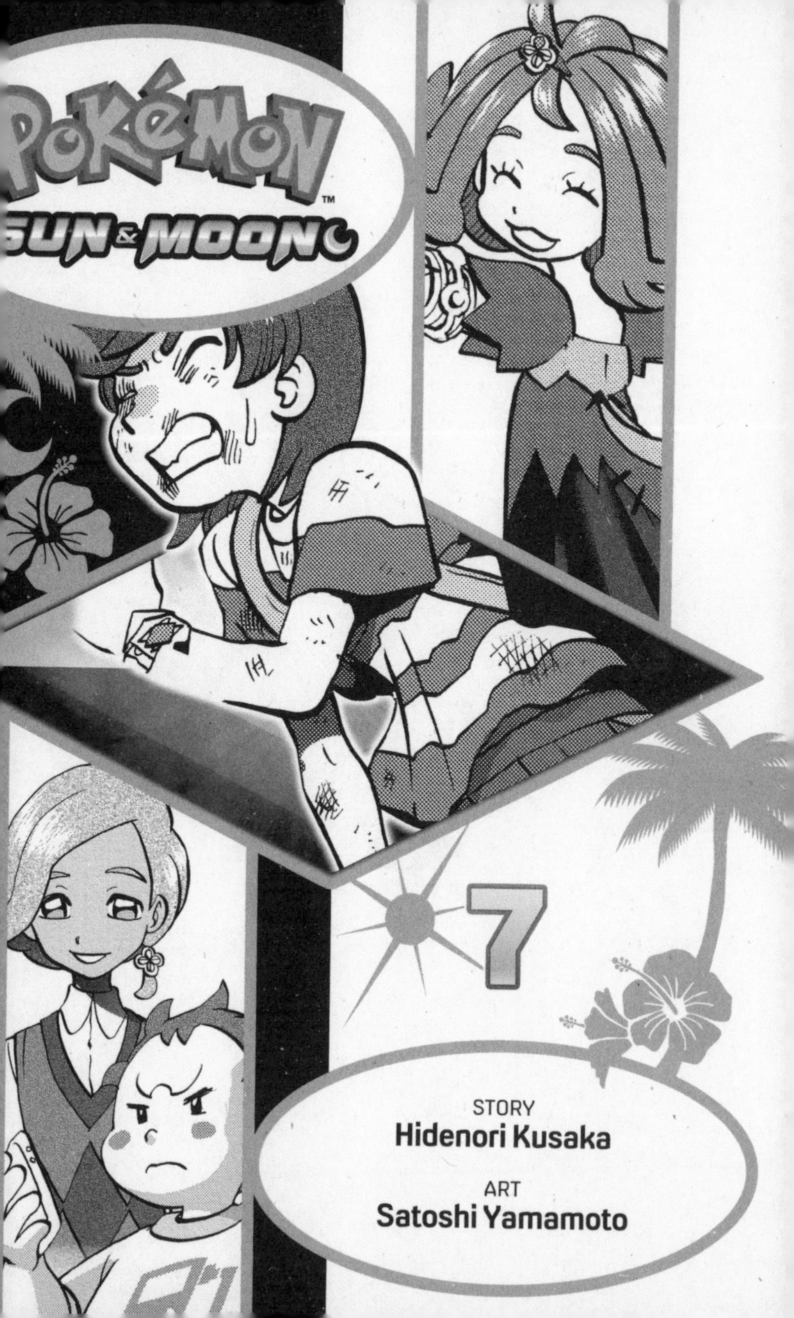

7

STORY
Hidenori Kusaka

ART
Satoshi Yamamoto

Introduction

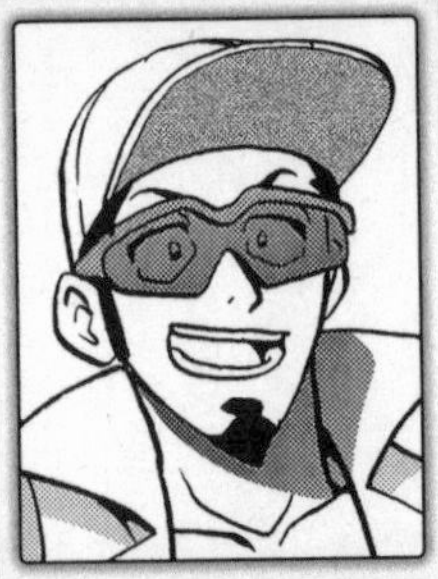

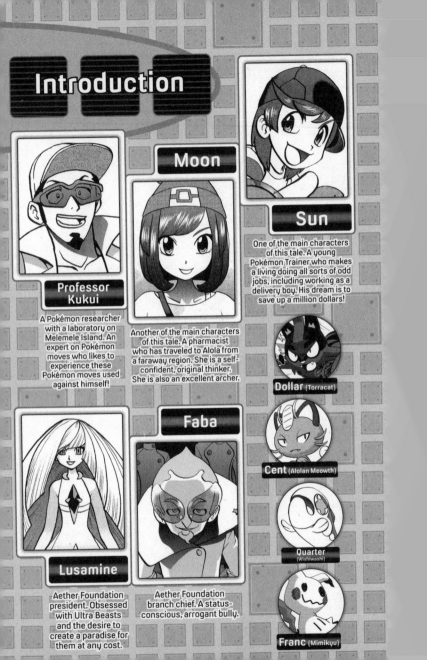

Professor Kukui

A Pokémon researcher with a laboratory on Melemele Island. An expert on Pokémon moves who likes to experience these Pokémon moves used against himself!

Moon

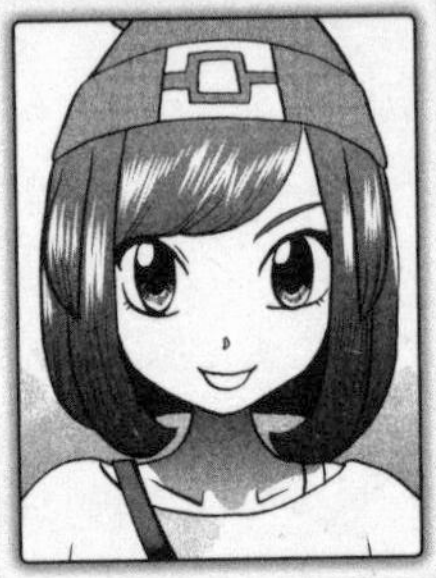

Another of the main characters of this tale. A pharmacist who has traveled to Alola from a faraway region. She is a self-confident, original thinker. She is also an excellent archer.

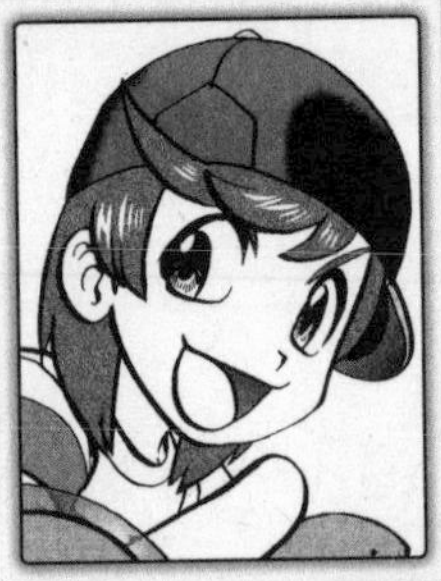

Sun

One of the main characters of this tale. A young Pokémon Trainer who makes a living doing all sorts of odd jobs, including working as a delivery boy. His dream is to save up a million dollars!

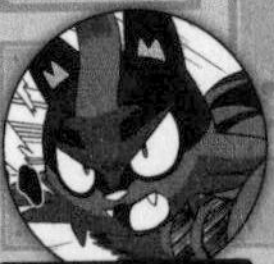

Dollar (Torracat)

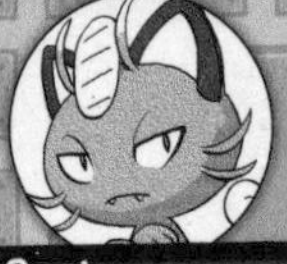

Cent (Alolan Meowth)

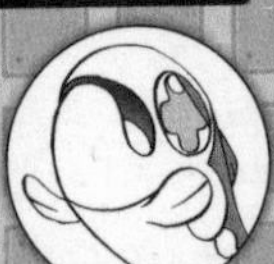

Quarter (Wishiwashi)

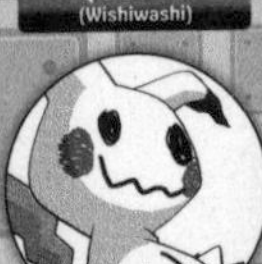

Franc (Mimikyu)

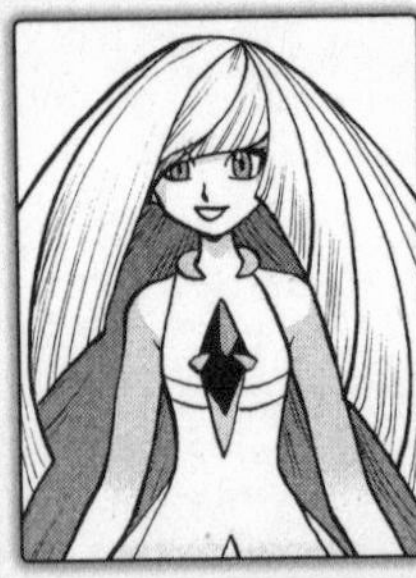

Lusamine

Aether Foundation president. Obsessed with Ultra Beasts and the desire to create a paradise for them at any cost.

Faba

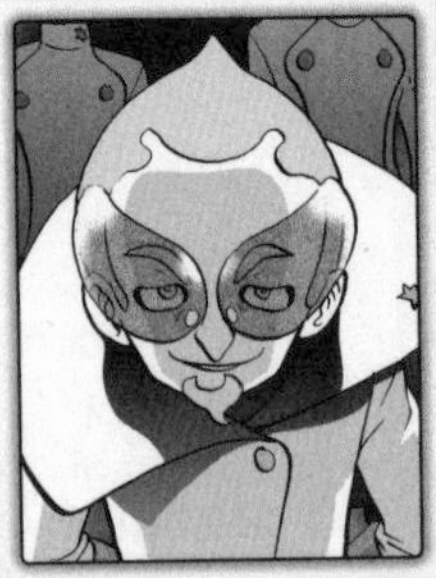

Aether Foundation branch chief. A status-conscious, arrogant bully.

Character

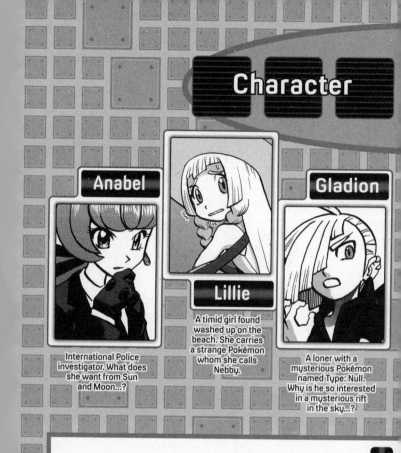

Anabel

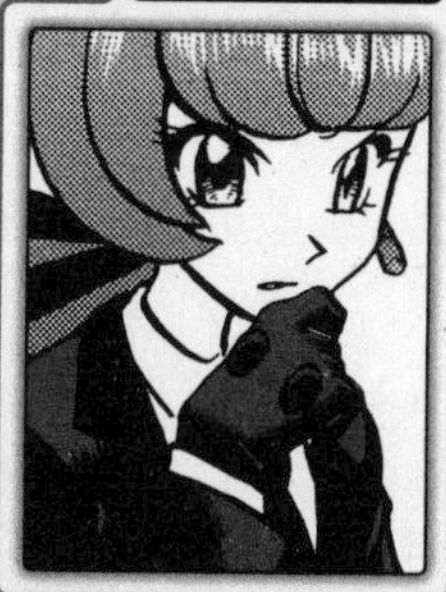

International Police investigator. What does she want from Sun and Moon...?

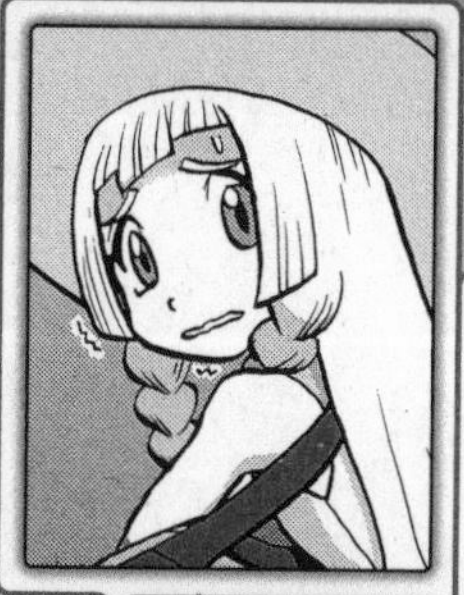

Lillie

A timid girl found washed up on the beach. She carries a strange Pokémon whom she calls Nebby.

Gladion

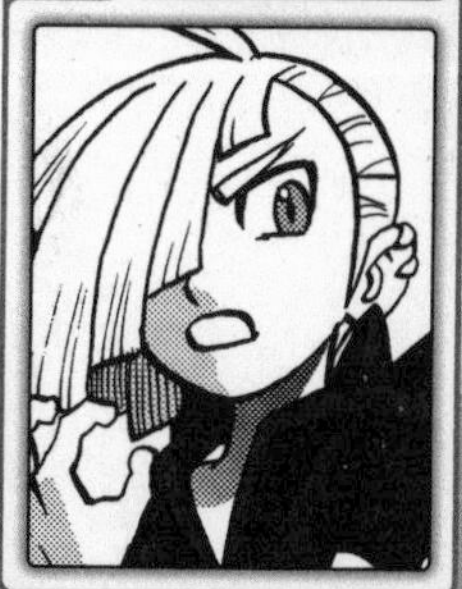

A loner with a mysterious Pokémon named Type: Null. Why is he so interested in a mysterious rift in the sky...?

The Story Thus Far...

Moon and Sun meet in the Alola region, a flower-filled vacation paradise, and end up traveling together to Professor Kukui's laboratory.

Since their arrival, the guardians of the Alolan Islands, called Tapu, have become agitated. During the Full Power Festival, Sun is chosen to take on the Island Challenge to soothe the Tapu's anger. Moon decides to assist him. On their journey, they meet a mysterious girl named Lillie whose Pokémon, a Cosmog nicknamed Nebby, creates rifts in the sky. Ultra Beasts arrive through these portals from an alternate dimension, and one of them drags Guzma, the boss of the nefarious Team Skull, to the other side. Ultra Beasts are now creating havoc throughout the Alola region. As fierce battles rage on many fronts, two International Police officers appear before Sun and Moon with an unusual request...

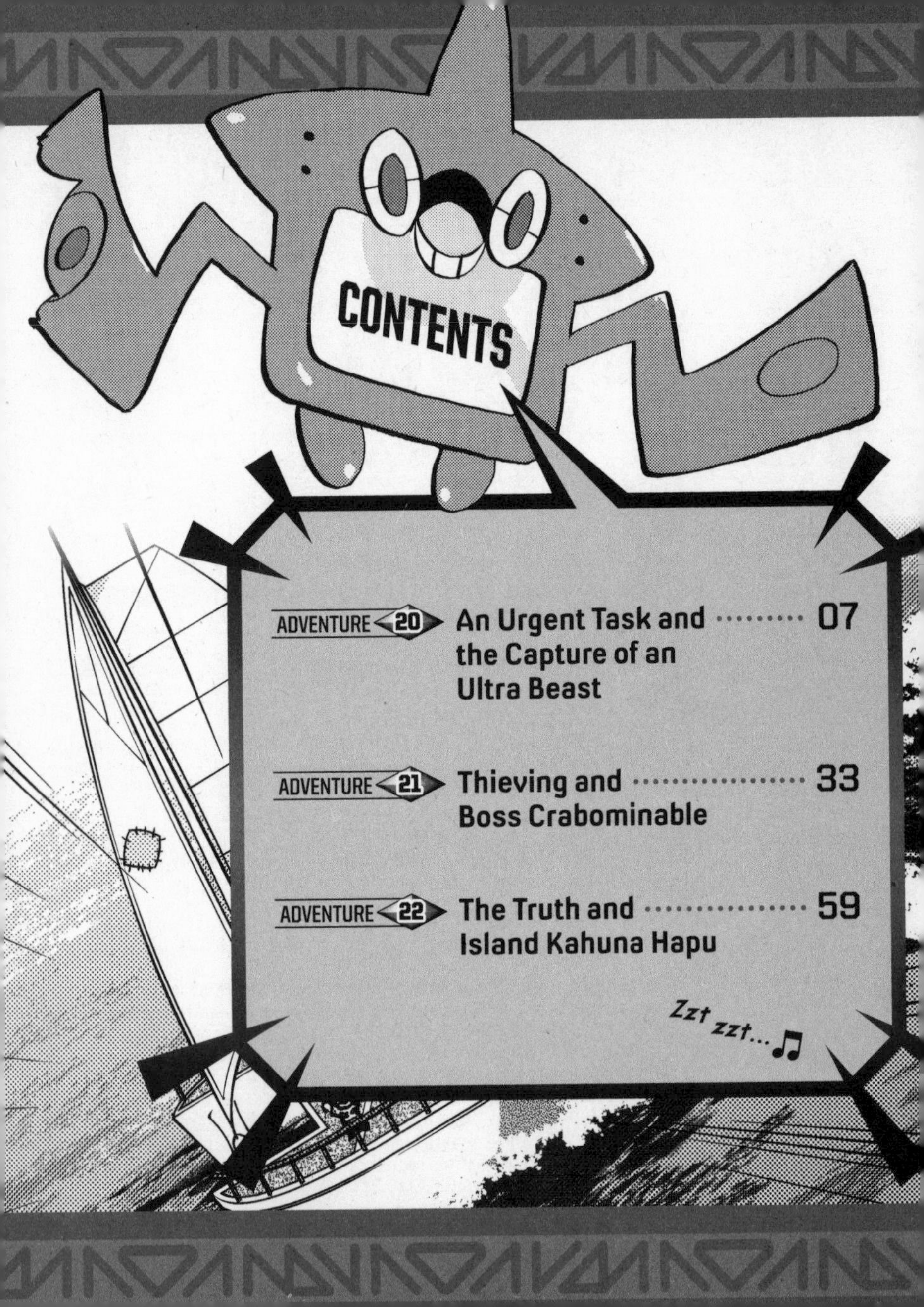
Zzt zzt...♫

CONTENTS

Adventure 20
An Urgent Task and the Capture of an Ultra Beast

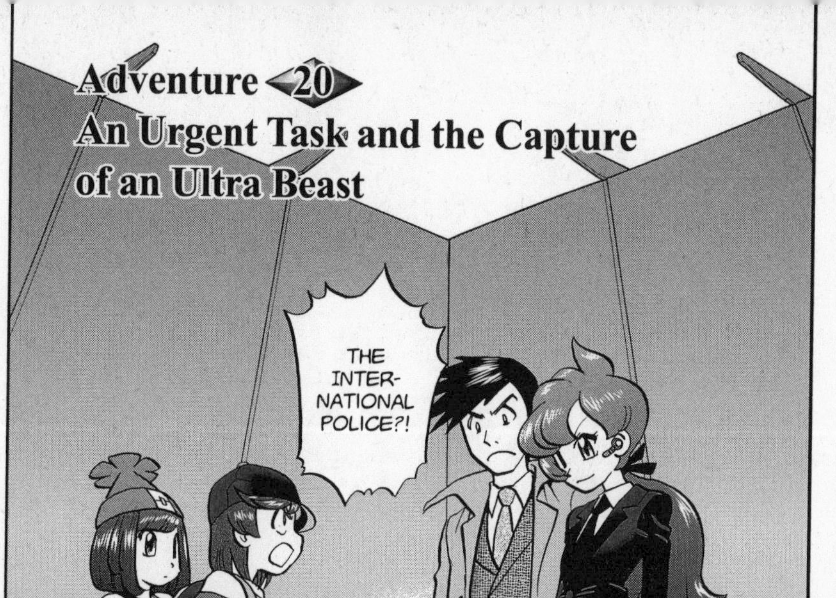
THE INTER-NATIONAL POLICE?!

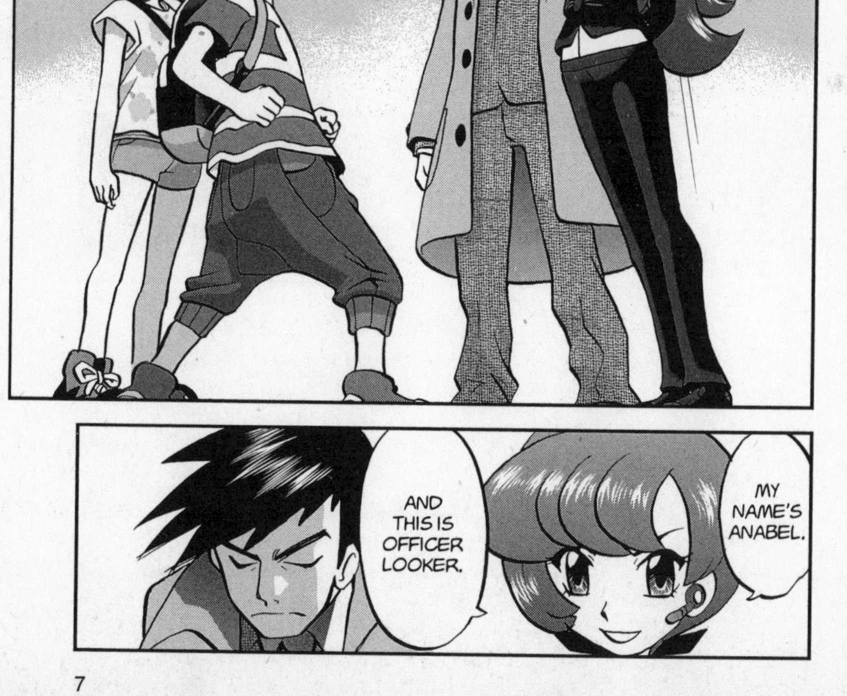
MY NAME'S ANABEL.
AND THIS IS OFFICER LOOKER.

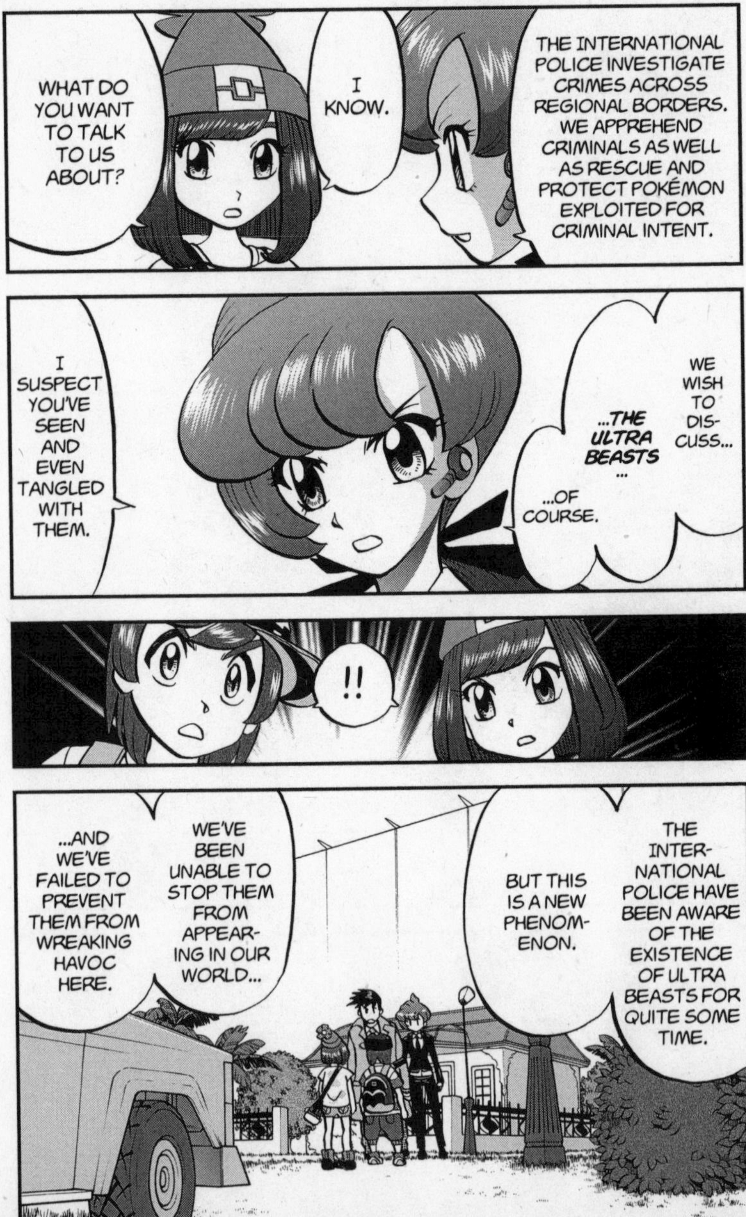
THE INTERNATIONAL POLICE INVESTIGATE CRIMES ACROSS REGIONAL BORDERS. WE APPREHEND CRIMINALS AS WELL AS RESCUE AND PROTECT POKÉMON EXPLOITED FOR CRIMINAL INTENT.
I KNOW.
WHAT DO YOU WANT TO TALK TO US ABOUT?
WE WISH TO DIS-CUSS...
...THE ULTRA BEASTS...
...OF COURSE.
I SUSPECT YOU'VE SEEN AND EVEN TANGLED WITH THEM.
!!
THE INTER-NATIONAL POLICE HAVE BEEN AWARE OF THE EXISTENCE OF ULTRA BEASTS FOR QUITE SOME TIME.
BUT THIS IS A NEW PHENOM-ENON.
WE'VE BEEN UNABLE TO STOP THEM FROM APPEAR-ING IN OUR WORLD...
...AND WE'VE FAILED TO PREVENT THEM FROM WREAKING HAVOC HERE.

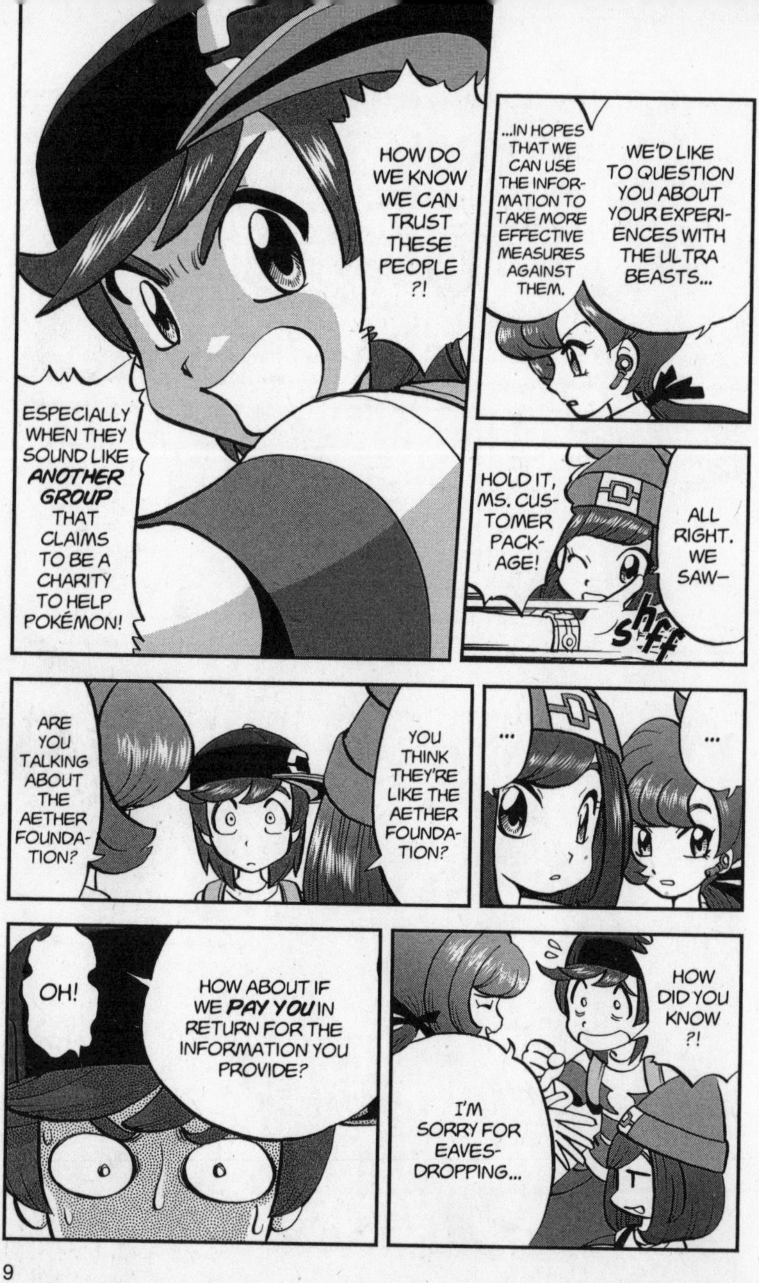
WE'D LIKE TO QUESTION YOU ABOUT YOUR EXPERIENCES WITH THE ULTRA BEASTS...
...IN HOPES THAT WE CAN USE THE INFORMATION TO TAKE MORE EFFECTIVE MEASURES AGAINST THEM.
ALL RIGHT. WE SAW—
HOLD IT, MS. CUSTOMER PACKAGE!
shff
HOW DO WE KNOW WE CAN TRUST THESE PEOPLE?!
ESPECIALLY WHEN THEY SOUND LIKE **ANOTHER GROUP** THAT CLAIMS TO BE A CHARITY TO HELP POKÉMON!
...
...
YOU THINK THEY'RE LIKE THE AETHER FOUNDATION?
ARE YOU TALKING ABOUT THE AETHER FOUNDATION?
HOW DID YOU KNOW?!
I'M SORRY FOR EAVESDROPPING...
HOW ABOUT IF WE **PAY YOU** IN RETURN FOR THE INFORMATION YOU PROVIDE?
OH!

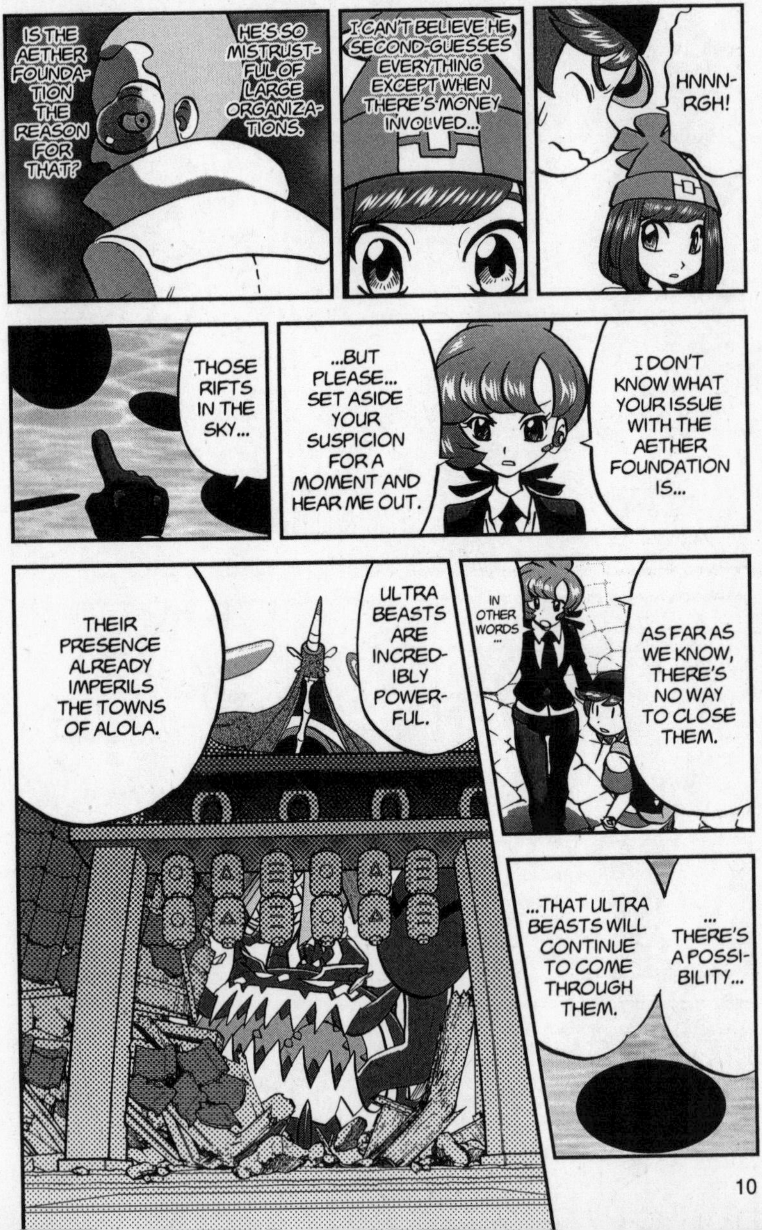
HNNN-RGH!
I CAN'T BELIEVE HE SECOND-GUESSES EVERYTHING EXCEPT WHEN THERE'S MONEY INVOLVED...
HE'S SO MISTRUST-FUL OF LARGE ORGANIZA-TIONS.
IS THE AETHER FOUNDA-TION THE REASON FOR THAT?
I DON'T KNOW WHAT YOUR ISSUE WITH THE AETHER FOUNDATION IS...
...BUT PLEASE... SET ASIDE YOUR SUSPICION FOR A MOMENT AND HEAR ME OUT.
THOSE RIFTS IN THE SKY...
AS FAR AS WE KNOW, THERE'S NO WAY TO CLOSE THEM.
IN OTHER WORDS...
... THERE'S A POSSI-BILITY...
...THAT ULTRA BEASTS WILL CONTINUE TO COME THROUGH THEM.
ULTRA BEASTS ARE INCRED-IBLY POWER-FUL.
THEIR PRESENCE ALREADY IMPERILS THE TOWNS OF ALOLA.

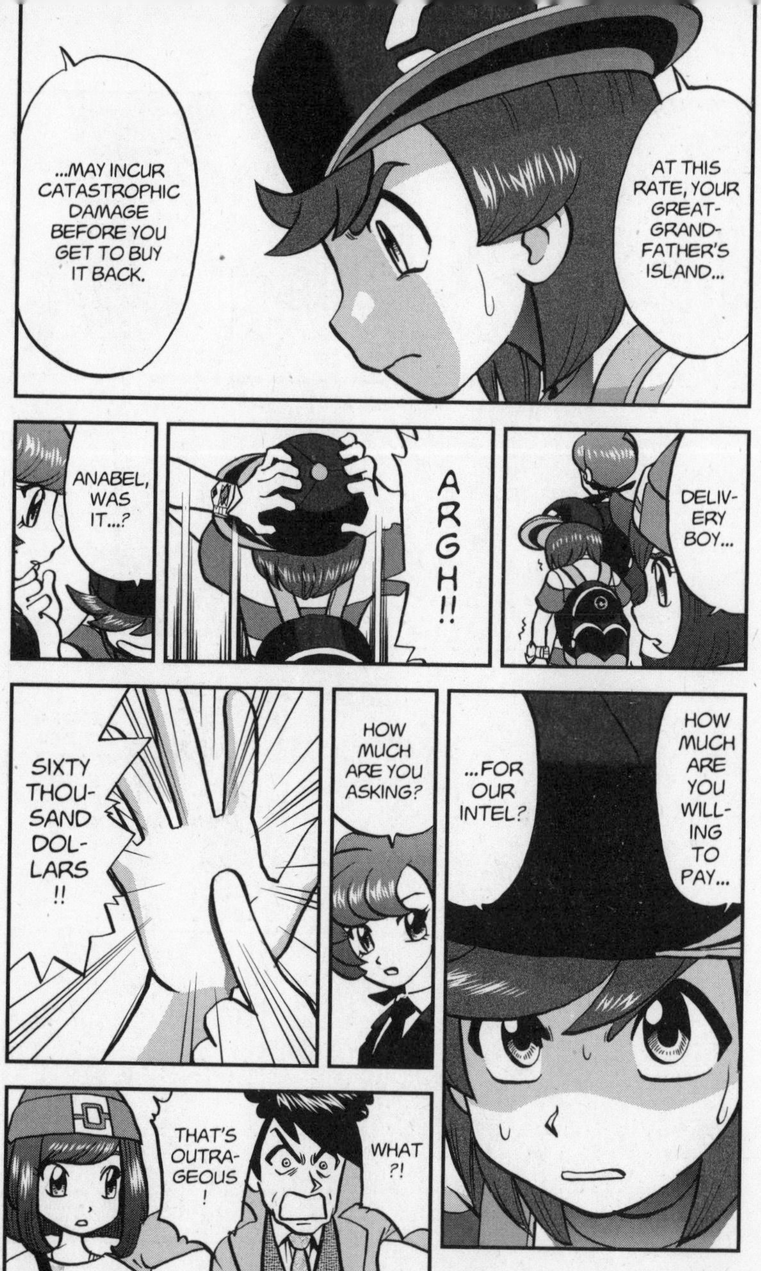
AT THIS RATE, YOUR GREAT-GRAND-FATHER'S ISLAND...
...MAY INCUR CATASTROPHIC DAMAGE BEFORE YOU GET TO BUY IT BACK.
DELIVERY BOY...
ARGH!!
ANABEL, WAS IT...?
HOW MUCH ARE YOU WILLING TO PAY...
...FOR OUR INTEL?
HOW MUCH ARE YOU ASKING?
SIXTY THOUSAND DOLLARS!!
WHAT?!
THAT'S OUTRAGEOUS!

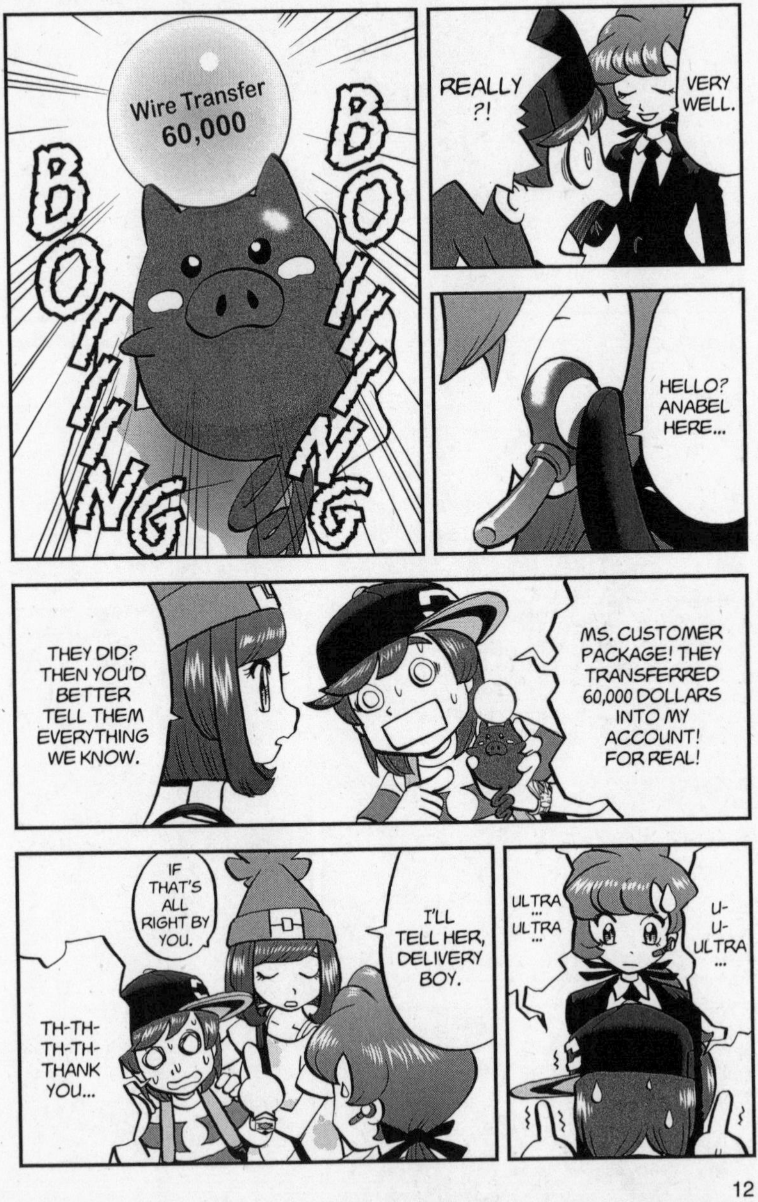
VERY WELL.
REALLY ?!
HELLO? ANABEL HERE...
BOING
Wire Transfer 60,000
BOING
MS. CUSTOMER PACKAGE! THEY TRANSFERRED 60,000 DOLLARS INTO MY ACCOUNT! FOR REAL!
THEY DID? THEN YOU'D BETTER TELL THEM EVERYTHING WE KNOW.
U-U-ULTRA...
ULTRA... ULTRA...
I'LL TELL HER, DELIVERY BOY.
IF THAT'S ALL RIGHT BY YOU.
TH-TH-TH-TH-THANK YOU...

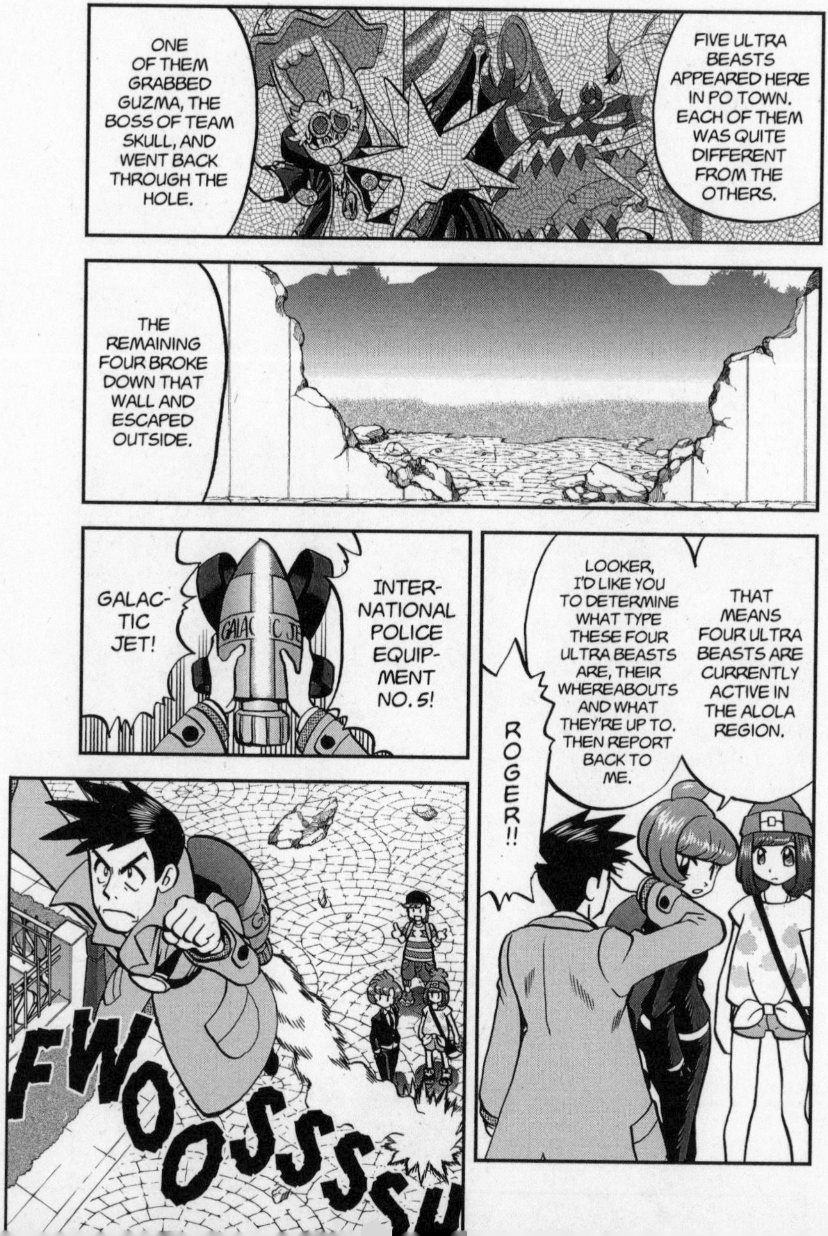
FIVE ULTRA BEASTS APPEARED HERE IN PO TOWN. EACH OF THEM WAS QUITE DIFFERENT FROM THE OTHERS.
ONE OF THEM GRABBED GUZMA, THE BOSS OF TEAM SKULL, AND WENT BACK THROUGH THE HOLE.
THE REMAINING FOUR BROKE DOWN THAT WALL AND ESCAPED OUTSIDE.
THAT MEANS FOUR ULTRA BEASTS ARE CURRENTLY ACTIVE IN THE ALOLA REGION.
LOOKER, I'D LIKE YOU TO DETERMINE WHAT TYPE THESE FOUR ULTRA BEASTS ARE, THEIR WHEREABOUTS AND WHAT THEY'RE UP TO. THEN REPORT BACK TO ME.
ROGER!!
INTER-NATIONAL POLICE EQUIP-MENT NO. 5!
GALAC-TIC JET!
GALACTIC JET
FWOOSSSH

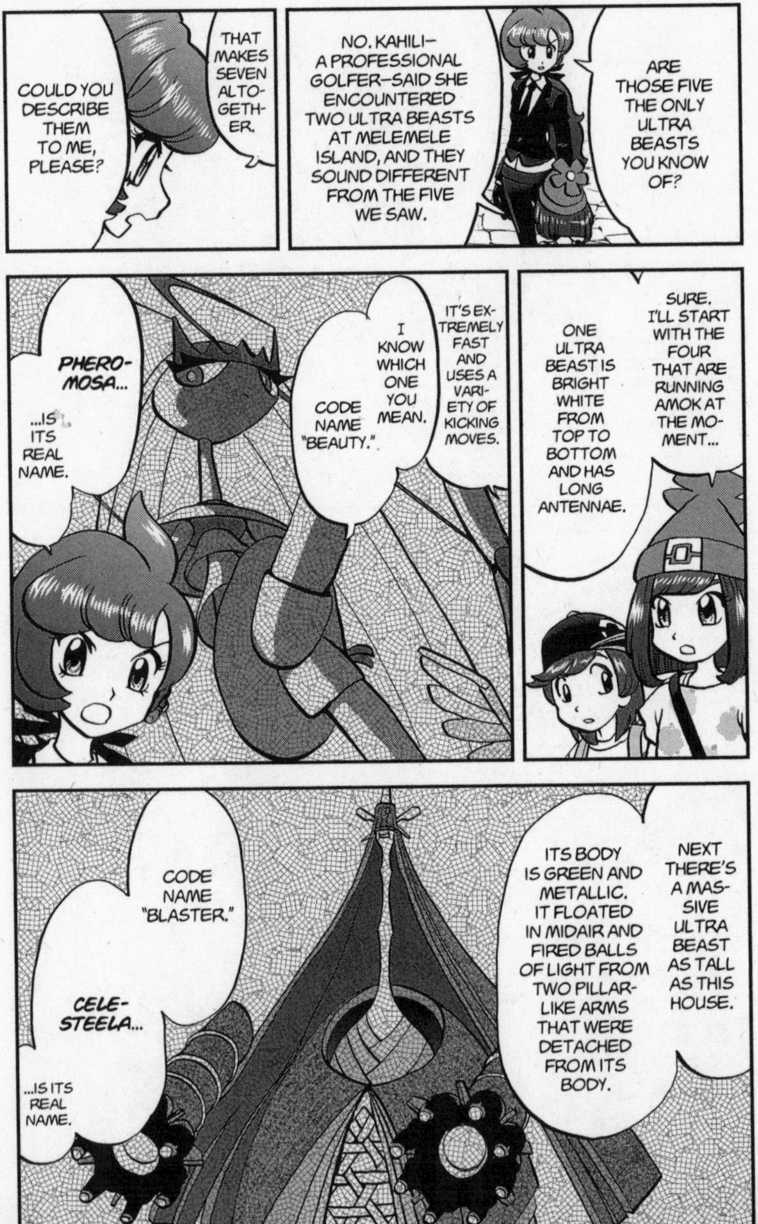
ARE THOSE FIVE THE ONLY ULTRA BEASTS YOU KNOW OF?
NO. KAHILI—A PROFESSIONAL GOLFER—SAID SHE ENCOUNTERED TWO ULTRA BEASTS AT MELEMELE ISLAND, AND THEY SOUND DIFFERENT FROM THE FIVE WE SAW.
THAT MAKES SEVEN ALTOGETHER.
COULD YOU DESCRIBE THEM TO ME, PLEASE?
SURE. I'LL START WITH THE FOUR THAT ARE RUNNING AMOK AT THE MOMENT...
ONE ULTRA BEAST IS BRIGHT WHITE FROM TOP TO BOTTOM AND HAS LONG ANTENNAE.
IT'S EXTREMELY FAST AND USES A VARIETY OF KICKING MOVES.
I KNOW WHICH ONE YOU MEAN.
CODE NAME "BEAUTY."
PHEROMOSA...
...IS ITS REAL NAME.
NEXT THERE'S A MASSIVE ULTRA BEAST AS TALL AS THIS HOUSE.
ITS BODY IS GREEN AND METALLIC. IT FLOATED IN MIDAIR AND FIRED BALLS OF LIGHT FROM TWO PILLAR-LIKE ARMS THAT WERE DETACHED FROM ITS BODY.
CODE NAME "BLASTER."
CELESTEELA...
...IS ITS REAL NAME.

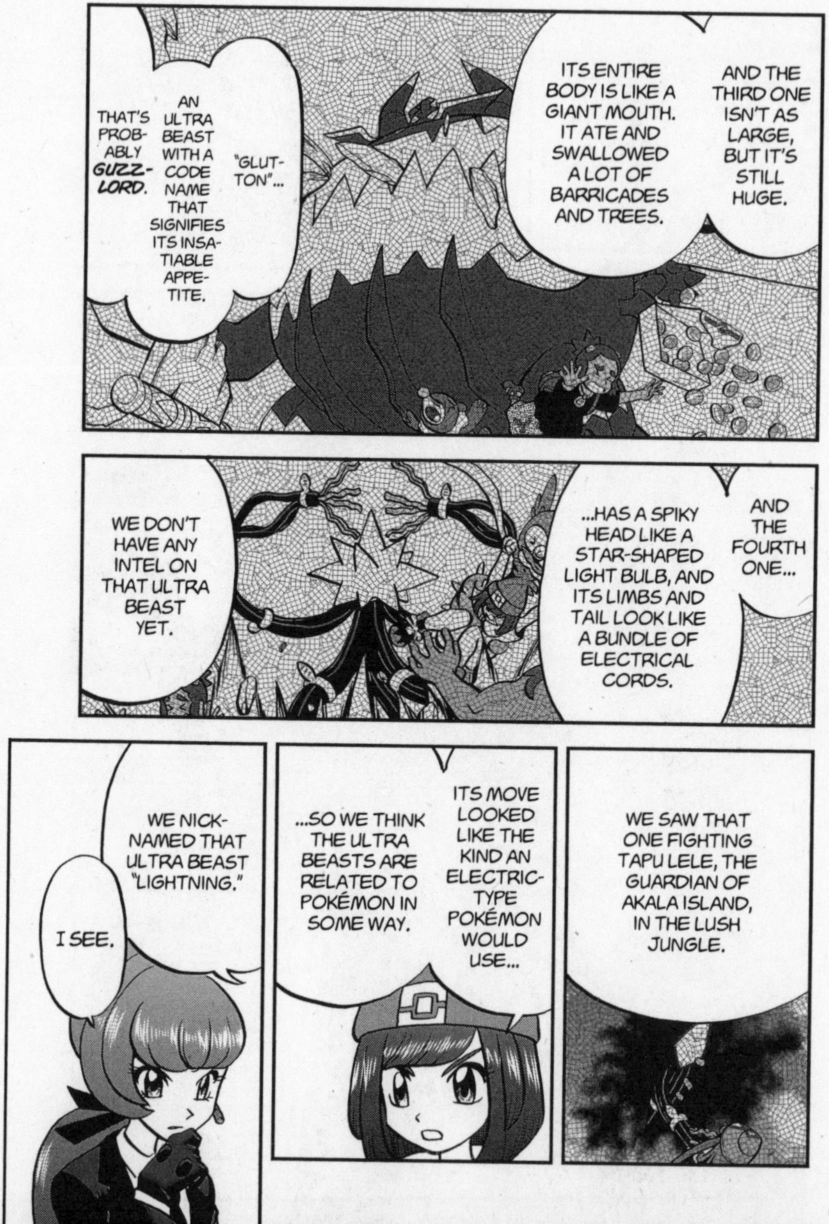

AND THE THIRD ONE ISN'T AS LARGE, BUT IT'S STILL HUGE.
ITS ENTIRE BODY IS LIKE A GIANT MOUTH. IT ATE AND SWALLOWED A LOT OF BARRICADES AND TREES.
"GLUT-TON"...
AN ULTRA BEAST WITH A CODE NAME THAT SIGNIFIES ITS INSA-TIABLE APPE-TITE.
THAT'S PROB-ABLY **GUZZ-LORD**.
AND THE FOURTH ONE...
...HAS A SPIKY HEAD LIKE A STAR-SHAPED LIGHT BULB, AND ITS LIMBS AND TAIL LOOK LIKE A BUNDLE OF ELECTRICAL CORDS.
WE DON'T HAVE ANY INTEL ON THAT ULTRA BEAST YET.
WE SAW THAT ONE FIGHTING TAPU LELE, THE GUARDIAN OF AKALA ISLAND, IN THE LUSH JUNGLE.
ITS MOVE LOOKED LIKE THE KIND AN ELECTRIC-TYPE POKÉMON WOULD USE...
...SO WE THINK THE ULTRA BEASTS ARE RELATED TO POKÉMON IN SOME WAY.
WE NICK-NAMED THAT ULTRA BEAST "LIGHTNING."
I SEE.

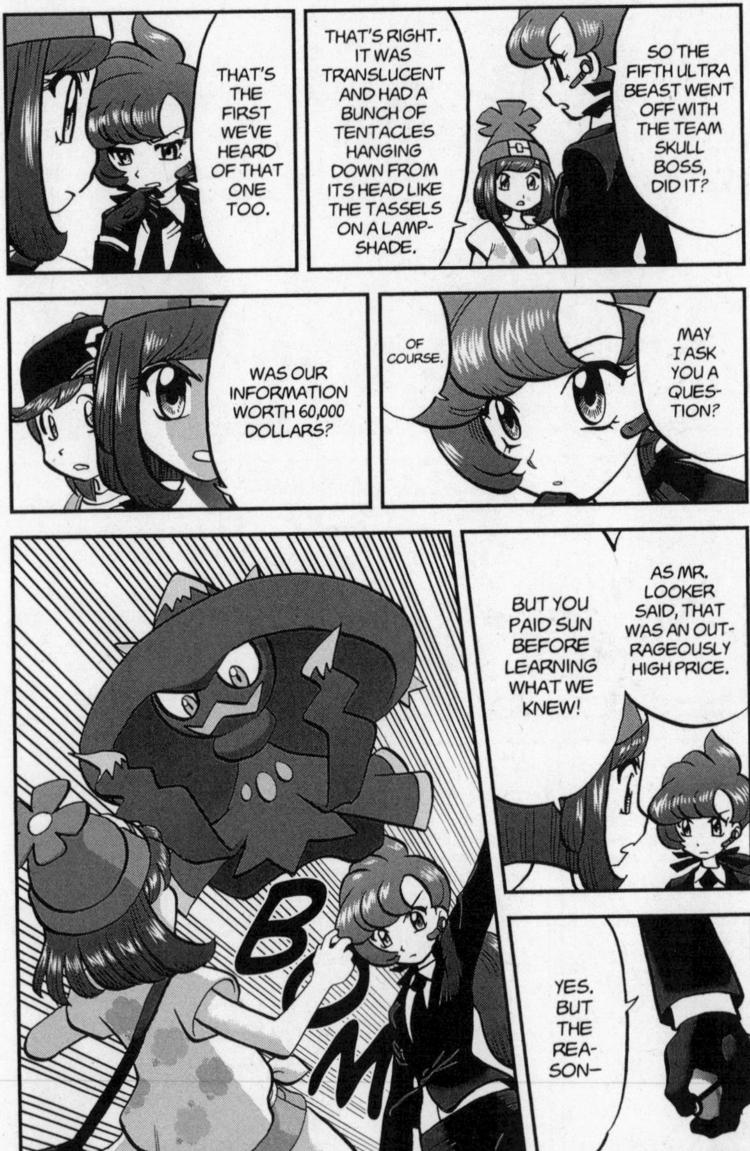
SO THE FIFTH ULTRA BEAST WENT OFF WITH THE TEAM SKULL BOSS, DID IT?
THAT'S RIGHT. IT WAS TRANSLUCENT AND HAD A BUNCH OF TENTACLES HANGING DOWN FROM ITS HEAD LIKE THE TASSELS ON A LAMP-SHADE.
THAT'S THE FIRST WE'VE HEARD OF THAT ONE TOO.
MAY I ASK YOU A QUES-TION?
OF COURSE.
WAS OUR INFORMATION WORTH 60,000 DOLLARS?
AS MR. LOOKER SAID, THAT WAS AN OUT-RAGEOUSLY HIGH PRICE.
BUT YOU PAID SUN BEFORE LEARNING WHAT WE KNEW!
YES. BUT THE REA-SON—

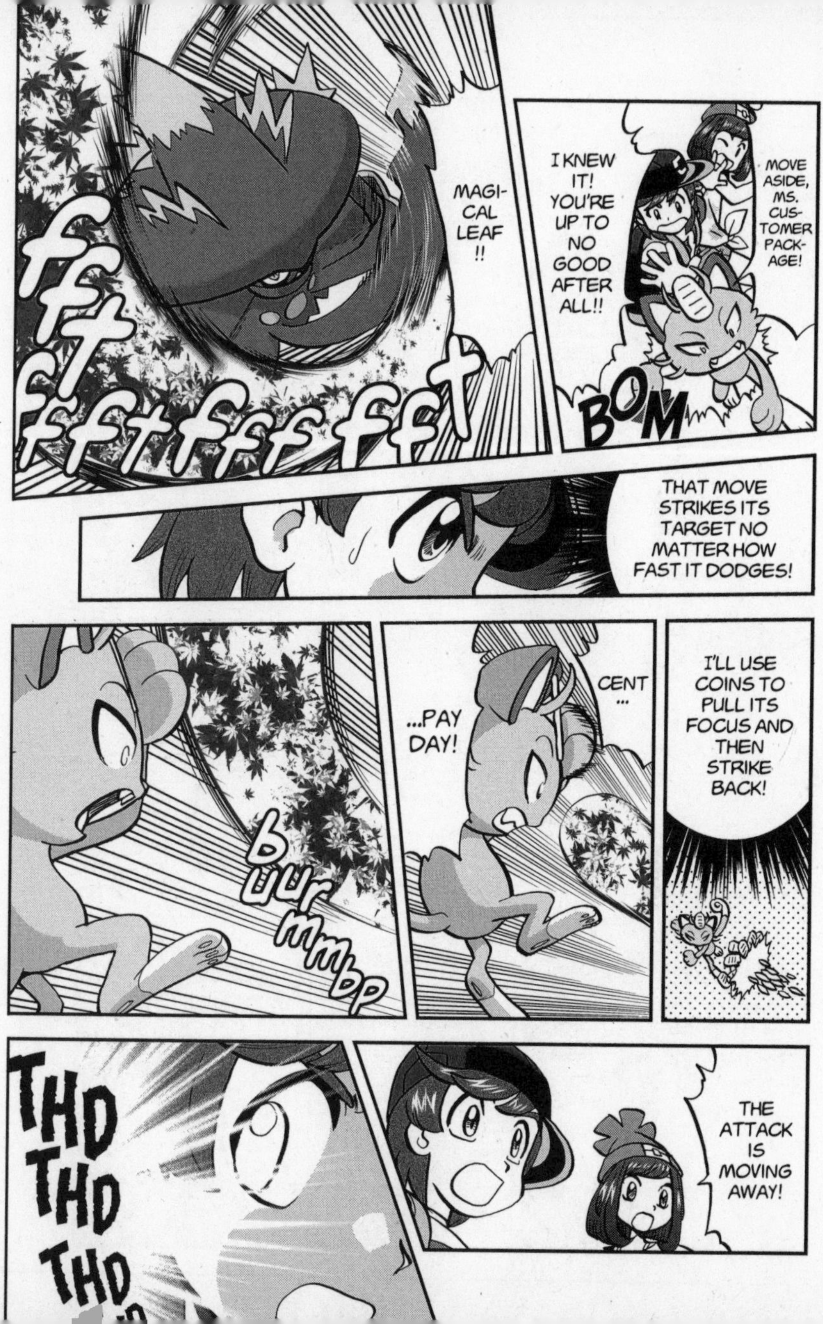
MOVE ASIDE, MS. CUSTOMER PACKAGE!
I KNEW IT! YOU'RE UP TO NO GOOD AFTER ALL!!
BOM
MAGICAL LEAF!!
ffffffffffffft
THAT MOVE STRIKES ITS TARGET NO MATTER HOW FAST IT DODGES!
I'LL USE COINS TO PULL ITS FOCUS AND THEN STRIKE BACK!
CENT...
...PAY DAY!
buurmmbp
THE ATTACK IS MOVING AWAY!
THD THD THD

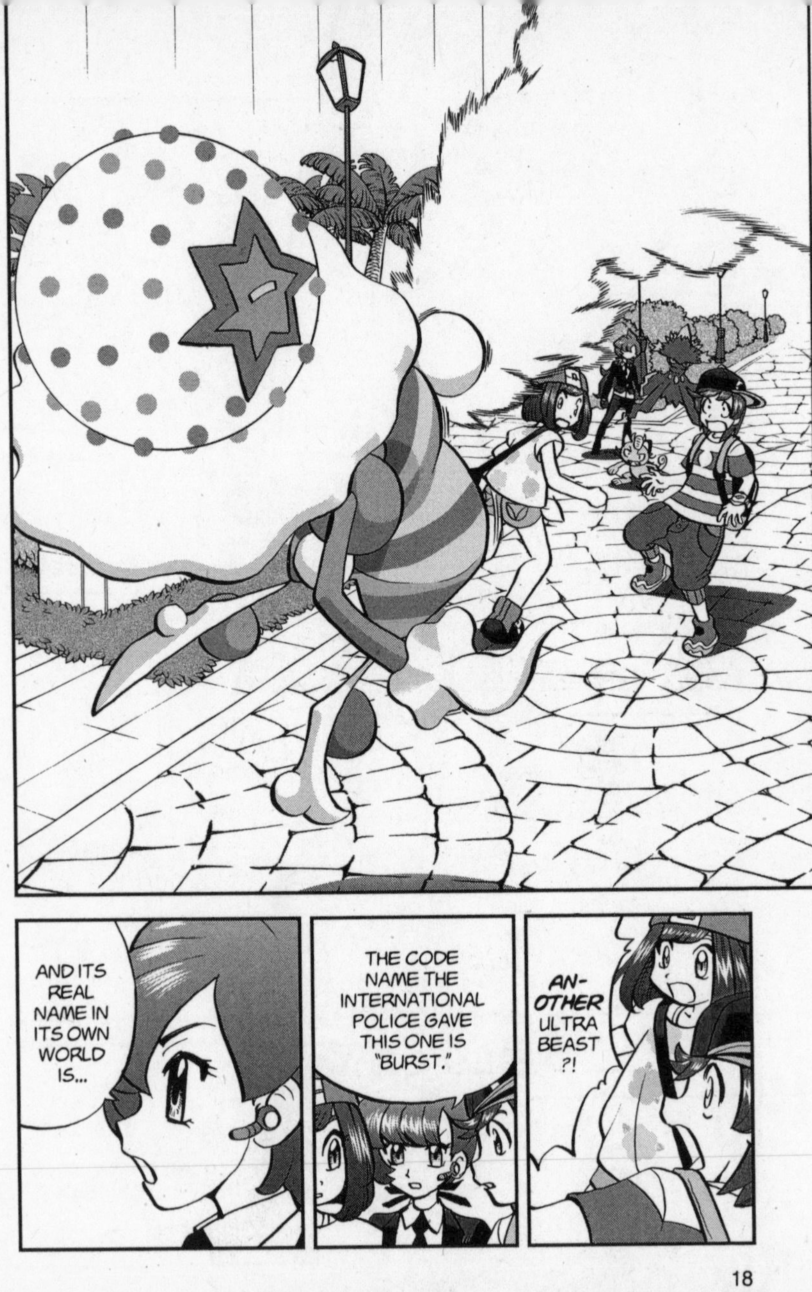
AN-OTHER ULTRA BEAST ?!
THE CODE NAME THE INTERNATIONAL POLICE GAVE THIS ONE IS "BURST."
AND ITS REAL NAME IN ITS OWN WORLD IS...

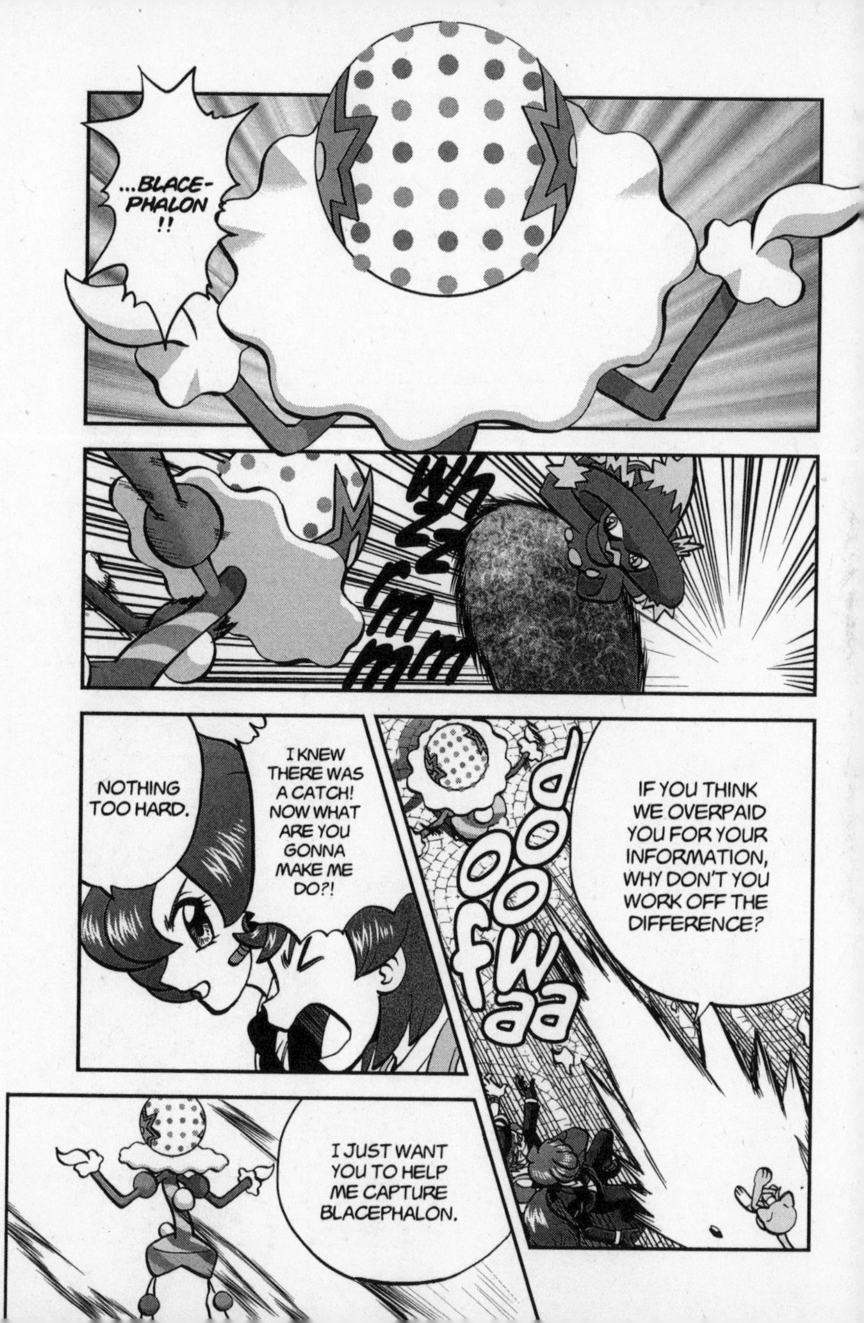
...BLACE-PHALON!!
IF YOU THINK WE OVERPAID YOU FOR YOUR INFORMATION, WHY DON'T YOU WORK OFF THE DIFFERENCE?
I KNEW THERE WAS A CATCH! NOW WHAT ARE YOU GONNA MAKE ME DO?!
NOTHING TOO HARD.
I JUST WANT YOU TO HELP ME CAPTURE BLACEPHALON.

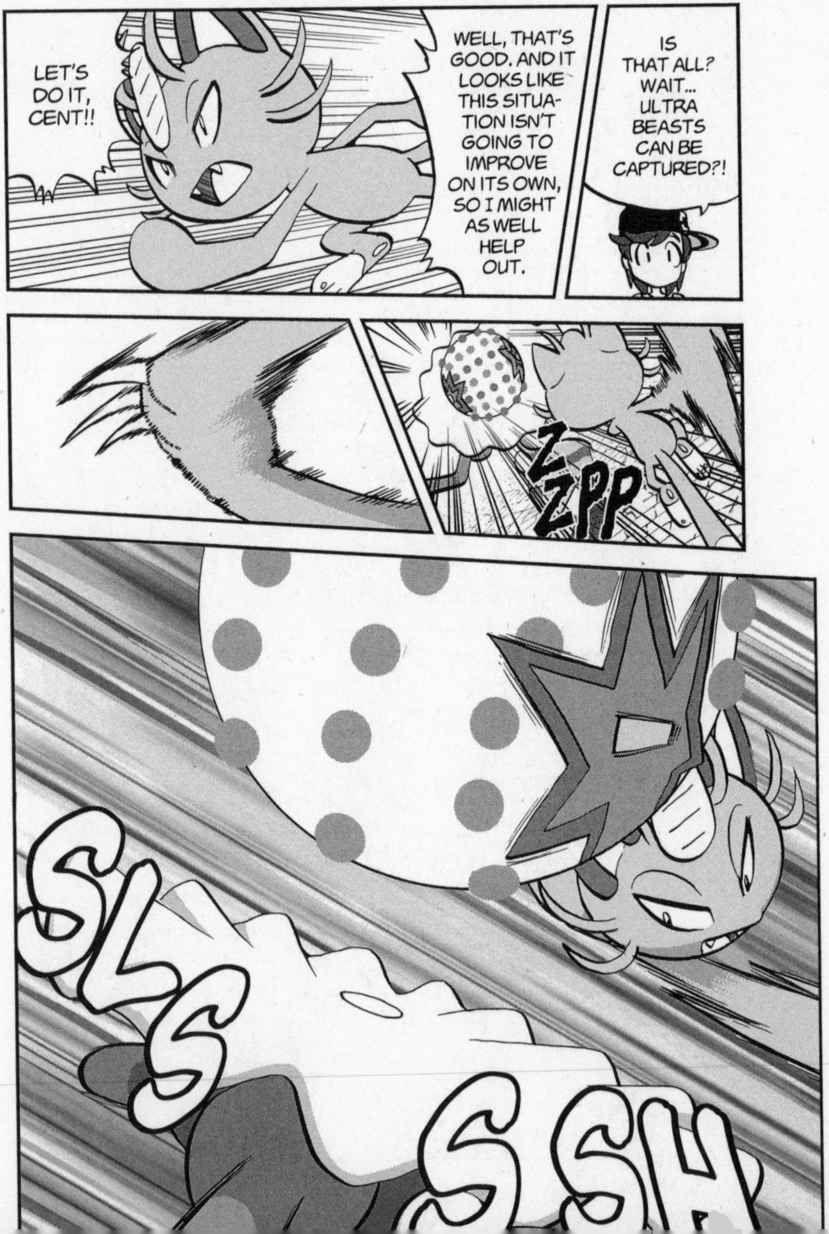
IS THAT ALL? WAIT... ULTRA BEASTS CAN BE CAPTURED?!
WELL, THAT'S GOOD. AND IT LOOKS LIKE THIS SITUATION ISN'T GOING TO IMPROVE ON ITS OWN, SO I MIGHT AS WELL HELP OUT.
LET'S DO IT, CENT!!
ZZPP
SLS
SSH

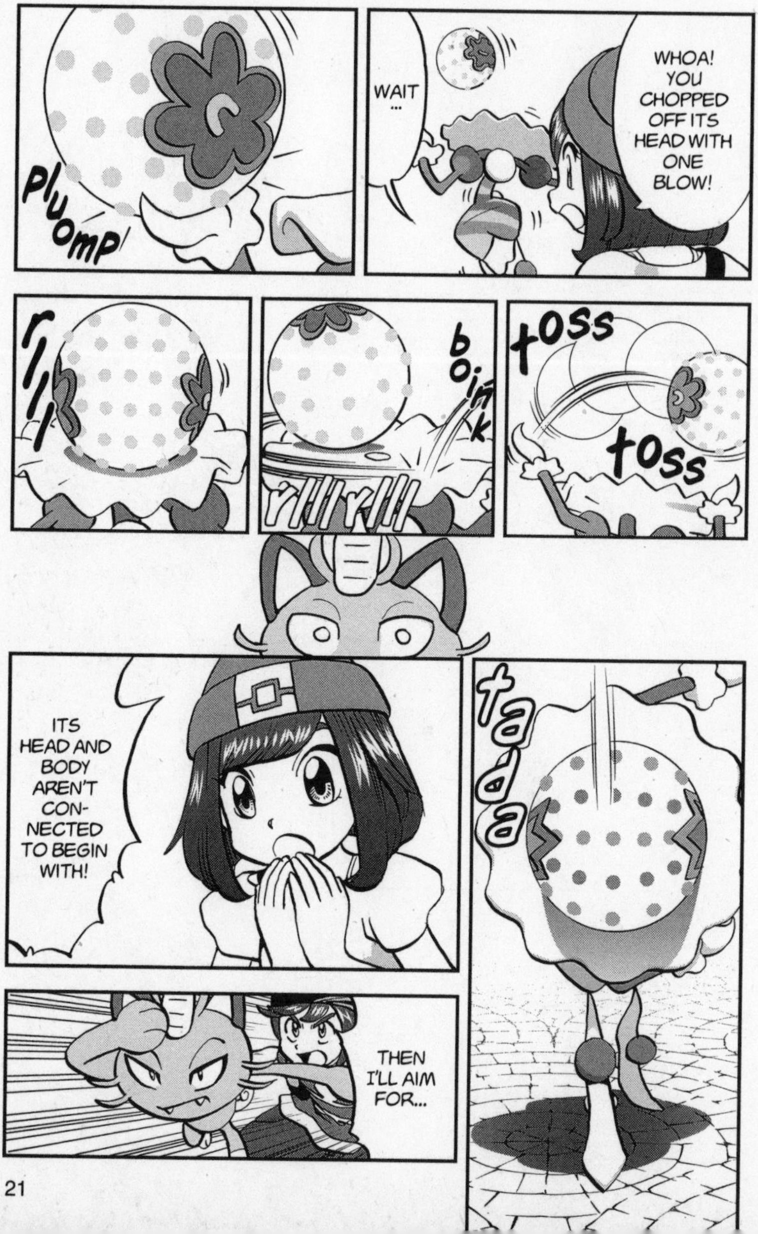
WHOA! YOU CHOPPED OFF ITS HEAD WITH ONE BLOW!
WAIT...
pluomp
toss
toss
boink
tada
ITS HEAD AND BODY AREN'T CON-NECTED TO BEGIN WITH!
THEN I'LL AIM FOR...

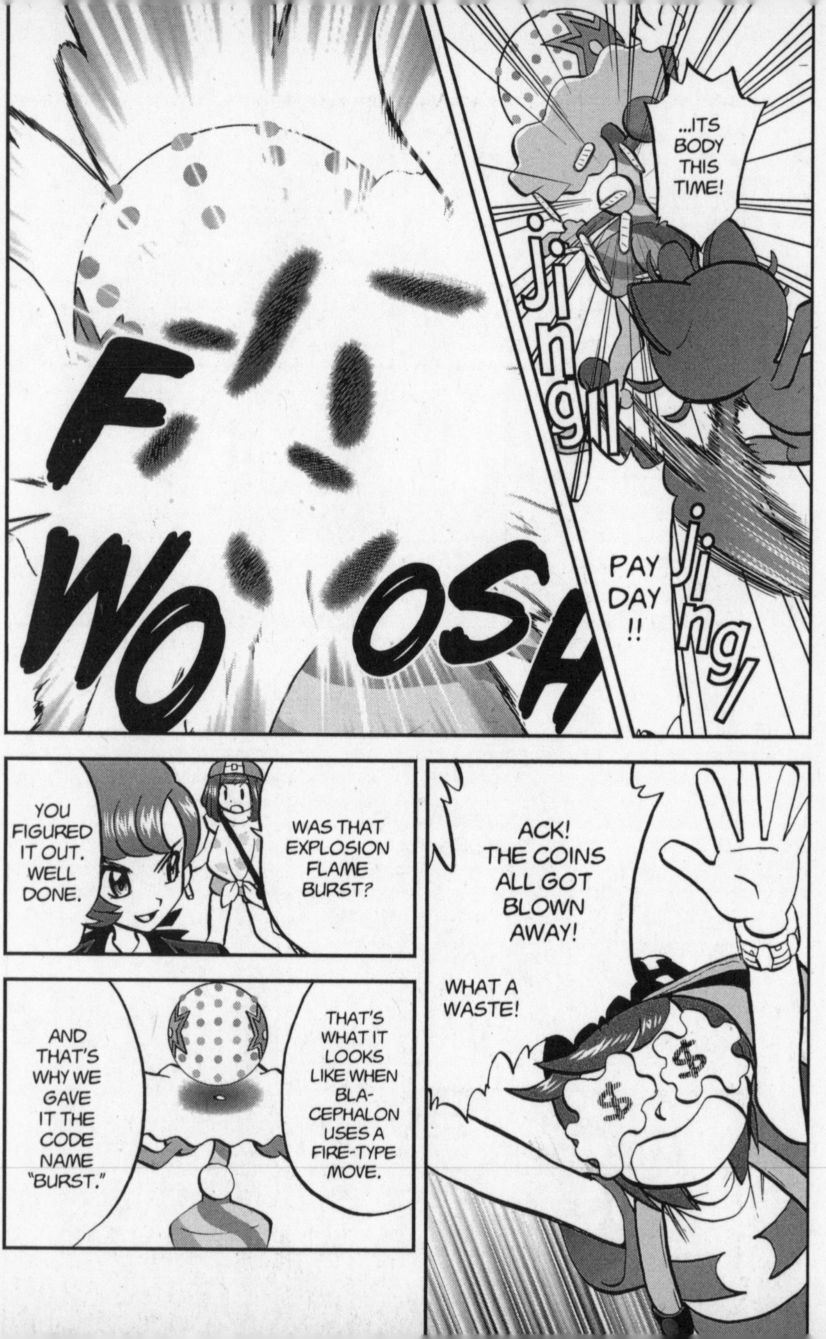
...ITS BODY THIS TIME!
Jingl
Jingl
PAY DAY !!
FWOOSH
ACK! THE COINS ALL GOT BLOWN AWAY!
WHAT A WASTE!
WAS THAT EXPLOSION FLAME BURST?
YOU FIGURED IT OUT. WELL DONE.
THAT'S WHAT IT LOOKS LIKE WHEN BLA-CEPHALON USES A FIRE-TYPE MOVE.
AND THAT'S WHY WE GAVE IT THE CODE NAME "BURST."

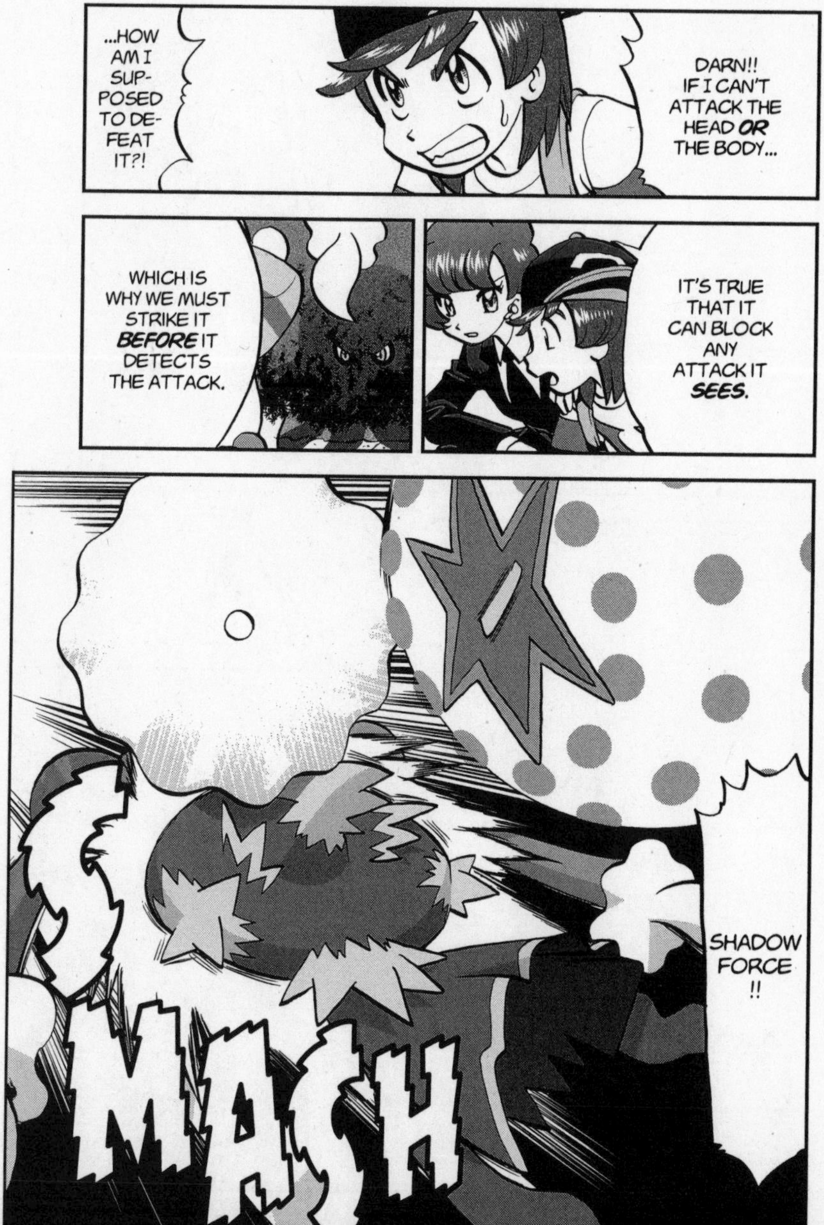
DARN!! IF I CAN'T ATTACK THE HEAD OR THE BODY...
...HOW AM I SUPPOSED TO DEFEAT IT?!
IT'S TRUE THAT IT CAN BLOCK ANY ATTACK IT SEES.
WHICH IS WHY WE MUST STRIKE IT BEFORE IT DETECTS THE ATTACK.
SHADOW FORCE !!
SMASH

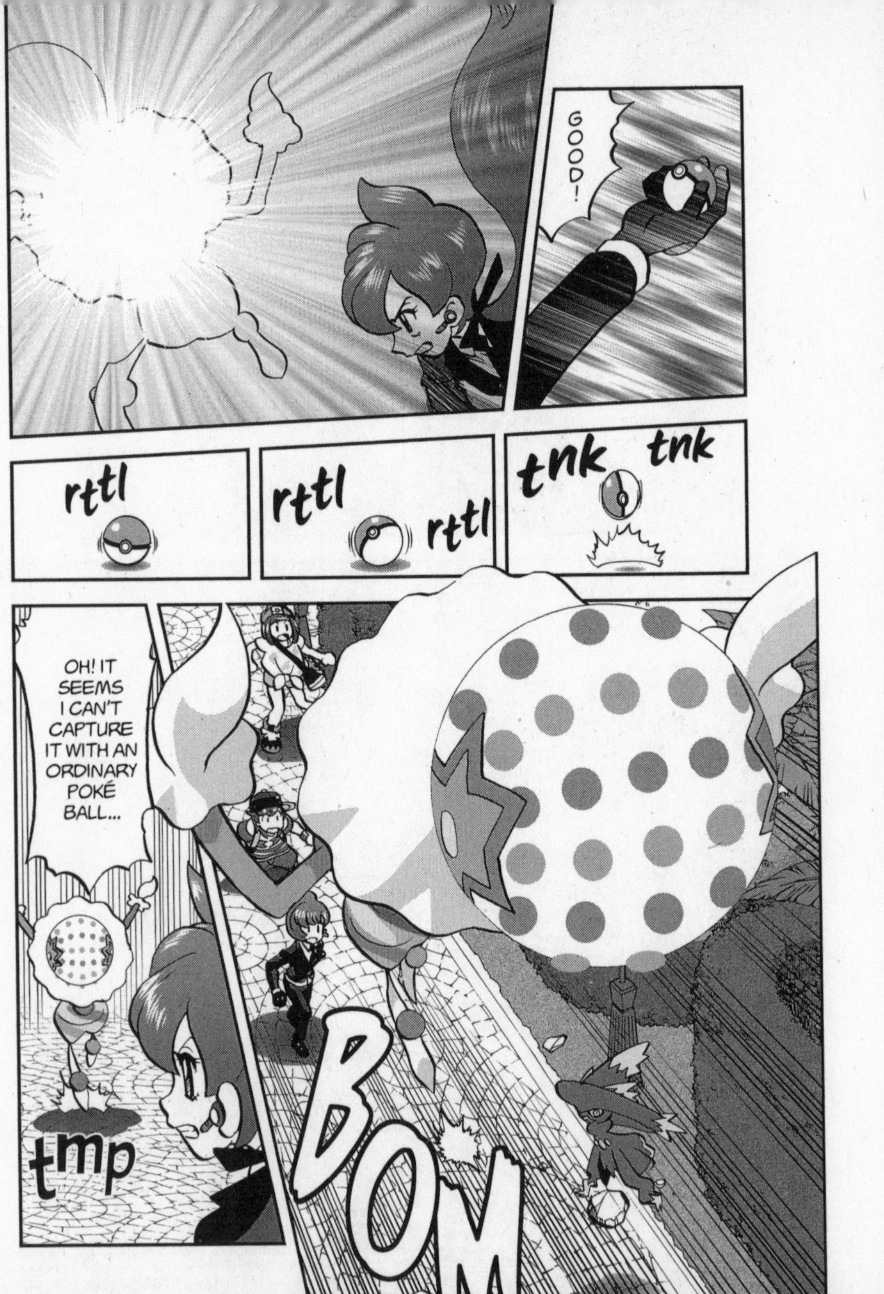
GOOD!
tnk tnk
rttl rttl
rttl
OH! IT SEEMS I CAN'T CAPTURE IT WITH AN ORDINARY POKÉ BALL...
BOM
tmp

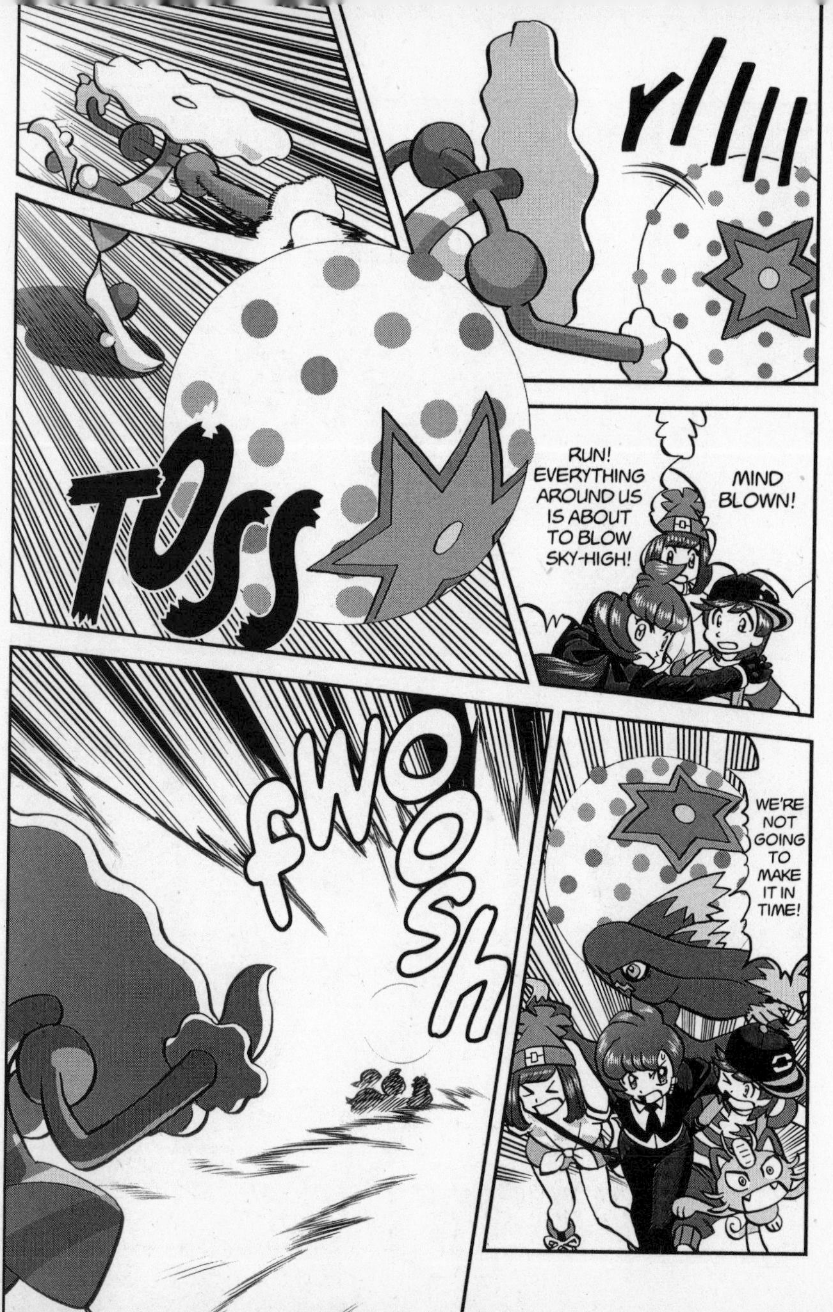
MIND BLOWN!
RUN! EVERYTHING AROUND US IS ABOUT TO BLOW SKY-HIGH!
TOSS
WE'RE NOT GOING TO MAKE IT IN TIME!
FWOOSH

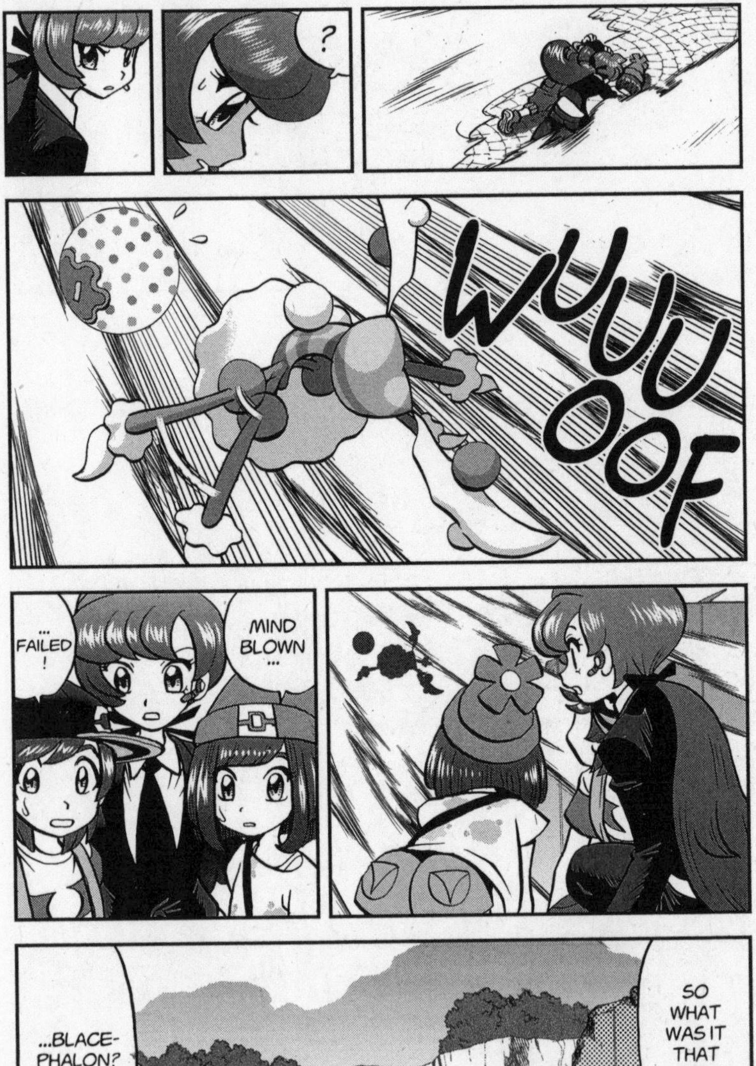
?
WUUUOOOF
MIND BLOWN ...
... FAILED !
SO WHAT WAS IT THAT BLEW AWAY...
...BLACE-PHALON?

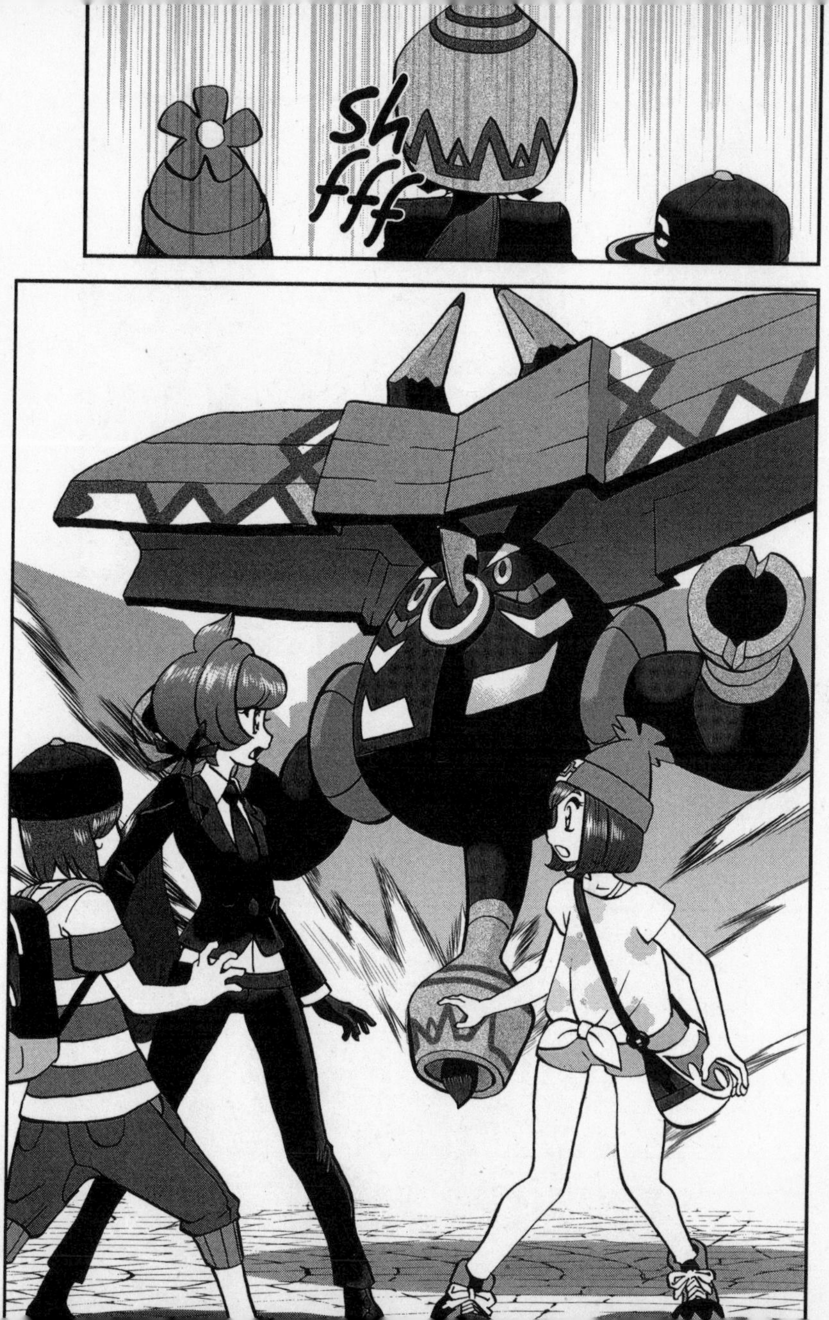
shfff

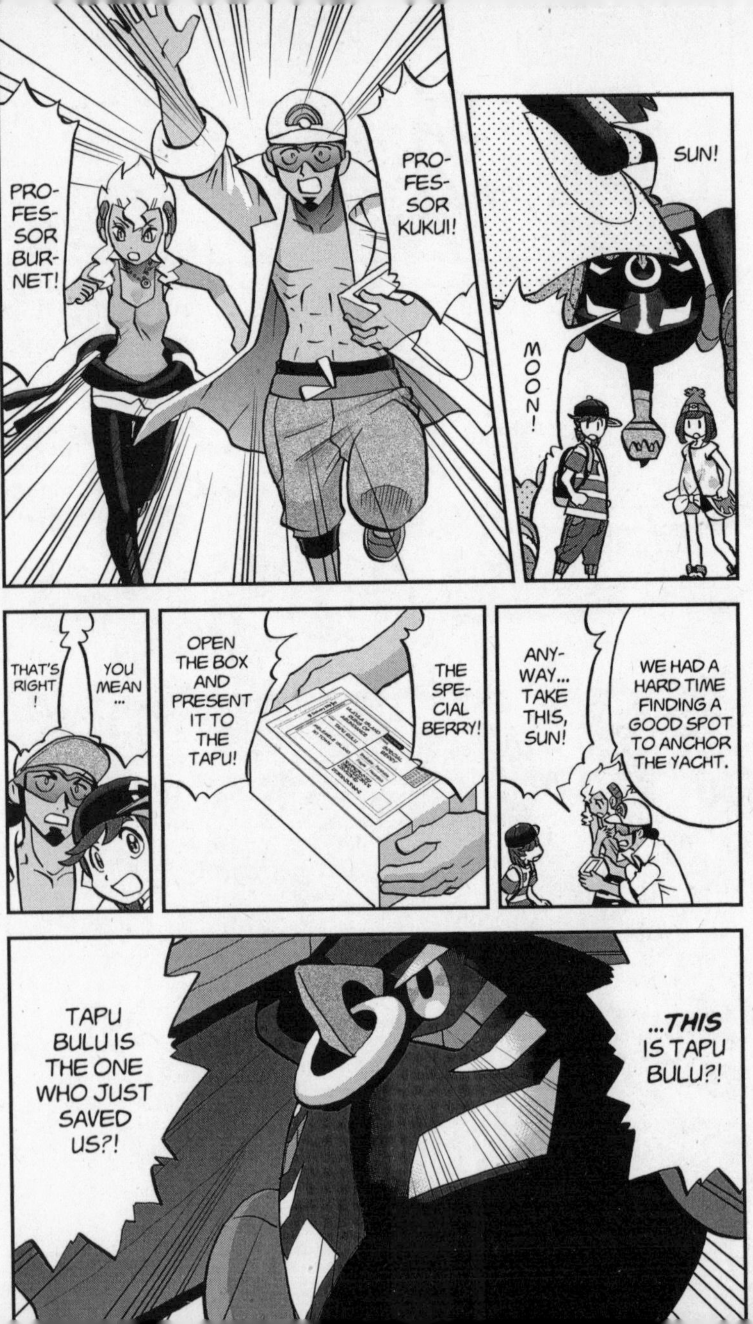
SUN!
MOON!
PROFESSOR KUKUI!
PROFESSOR BURNET!
WE HAD A HARD TIME FINDING A GOOD SPOT TO ANCHOR THE YACHT.
ANYWAY... TAKE THIS, SUN!
THE SPECIAL BERRY!
OPEN THE BOX AND PRESENT IT TO THE TAPU!
YOU MEAN...
THAT'S RIGHT!
...THIS IS TAPU BULU?!
TAPU BULU IS THE ONE WHO JUST SAVED US?!

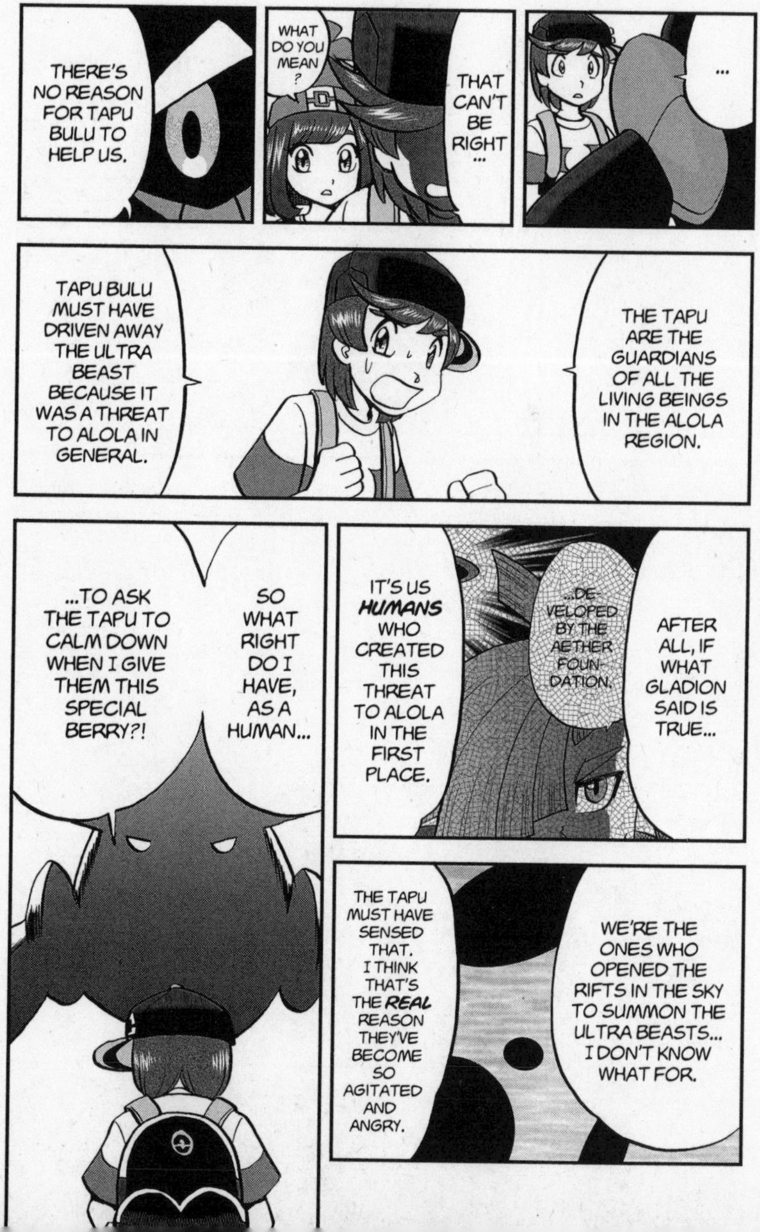
...
THAT CAN'T BE RIGHT...
WHAT DO YOU MEAN?
THERE'S NO REASON FOR TAPU BULU TO HELP US.
THE TAPU ARE THE GUARDIANS OF ALL THE LIVING BEINGS IN THE ALOLA REGION.
TAPU BULU MUST HAVE DRIVEN AWAY THE ULTRA BEAST BECAUSE IT WAS A THREAT TO ALOLA IN GENERAL.
AFTER ALL, IF WHAT GLADION SAID IS TRUE...
...DEVELOPED BY THE AETHER FOUNDATION.
IT'S US **HUMANS** WHO CREATED THIS THREAT TO ALOLA IN THE FIRST PLACE.
WE'RE THE ONES WHO OPENED THE RIFTS IN THE SKY TO SUMMON THE ULTRA BEASTS... I DON'T KNOW WHAT FOR.
THE TAPU MUST HAVE SENSED THAT. I THINK THAT'S THE **REAL** REASON THEY'VE BECOME SO AGITATED AND ANGRY.
SO WHAT RIGHT DO I HAVE, AS A HUMAN...
...TO ASK THE TAPU TO CALM DOWN WHEN I GIVE THEM THIS SPECIAL BERRY?!

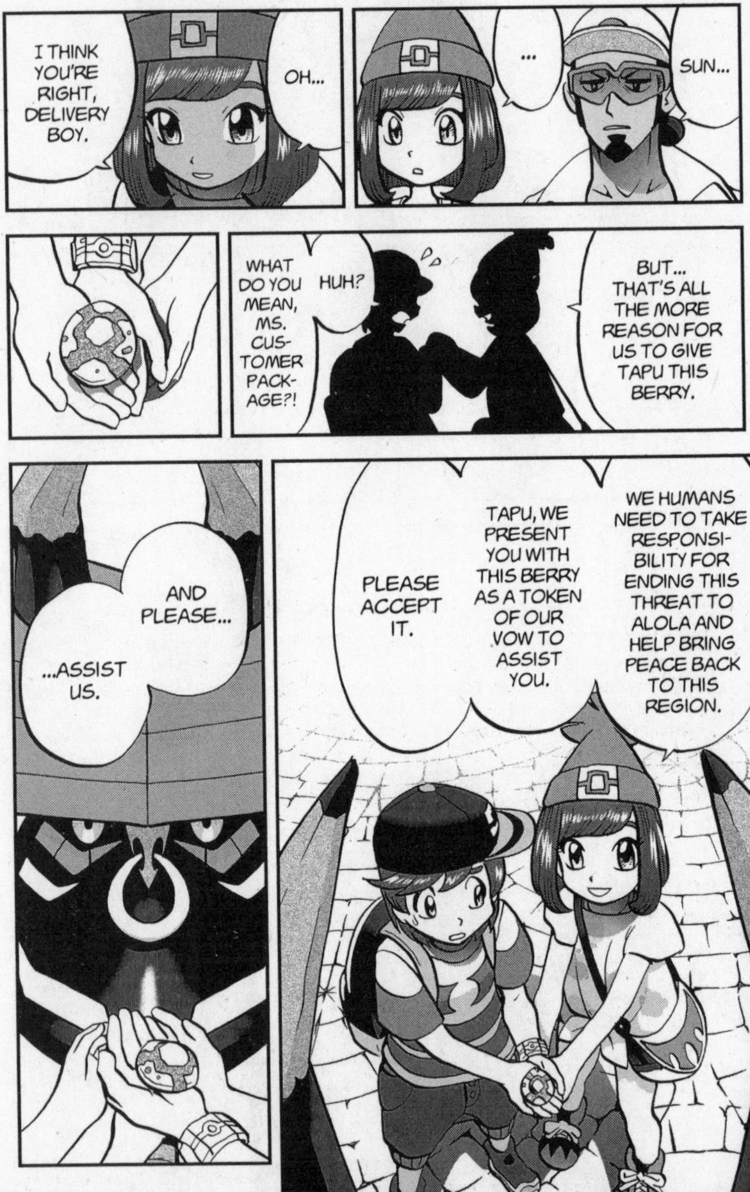
SUN...
...
OH...
I THINK YOU'RE RIGHT, DELIVERY BOY.
BUT... THAT'S ALL THE MORE REASON FOR US TO GIVE TAPU THIS BERRY.
HUH?
WHAT DO YOU MEAN, MS. CUS-TOMER PACK-AGE?!
WE HUMANS NEED TO TAKE RESPONSI-BILITY FOR ENDING THIS THREAT TO ALOLA AND HELP BRING PEACE BACK TO THIS REGION.
TAPU, WE PRESENT YOU WITH THIS BERRY AS A TOKEN OF OUR VOW TO ASSIST YOU.
PLEASE ACCEPT IT.
AND PLEASE...
...ASSIST US.

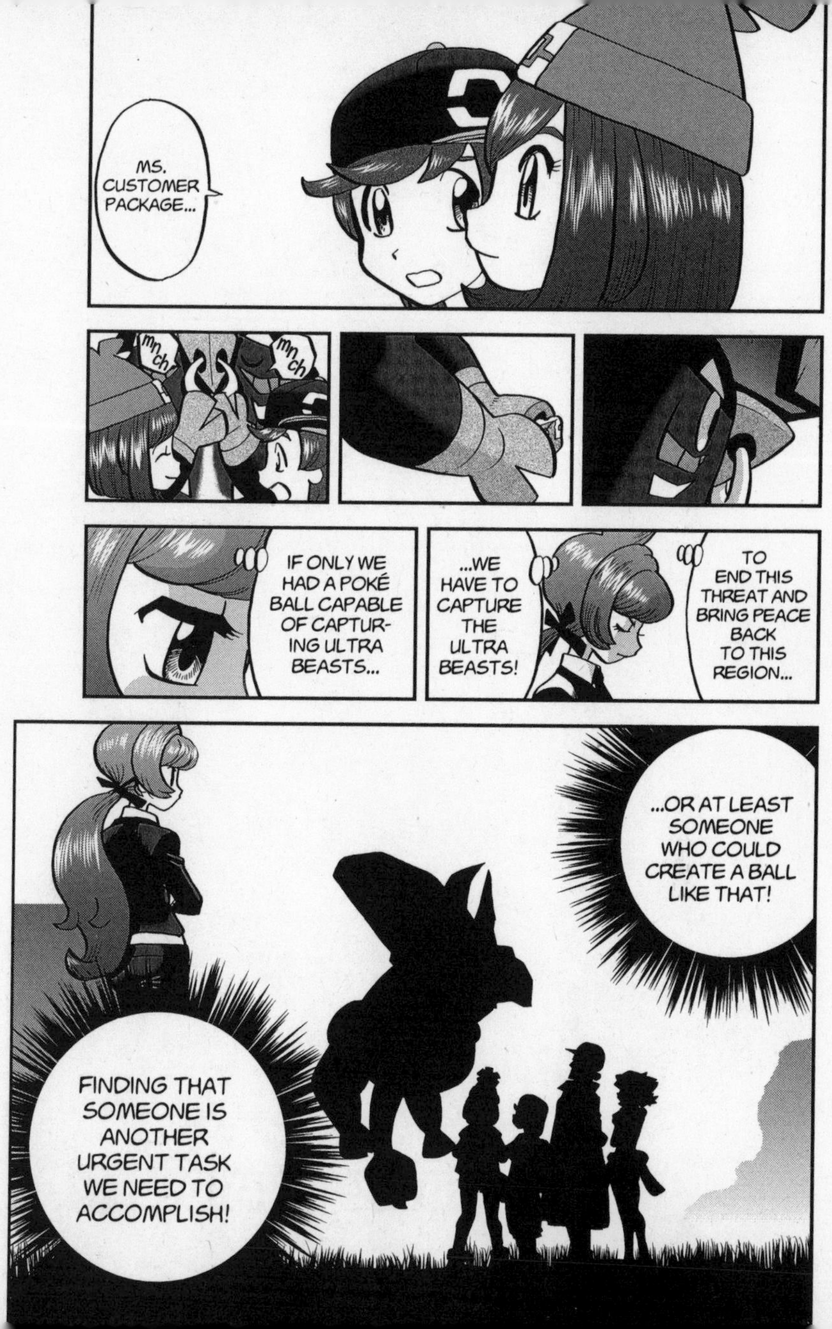
MS. CUSTOMER PACKAGE...
mnch
mnch
TO END THIS THREAT AND BRING PEACE BACK TO THIS REGION...
...WE HAVE TO CAPTURE THE ULTRA BEASTS!
IF ONLY WE HAD A POKÉ BALL CAPABLE OF CAPTURING ULTRA BEASTS...
...OR AT LEAST SOMEONE WHO COULD CREATE A BALL LIKE THAT!
FINDING THAT SOMEONE IS ANOTHER URGENT TASK WE NEED TO ACCOMPLISH!

The Four Islands

Melemele Island, Akala Island, Ula'ula Island and Poni Island. The Alola region consists of these four islands. People use ships and Mantine surfing to travel between them. The culture of the residents differs from island to island too.

♪

Guide to Alola 17

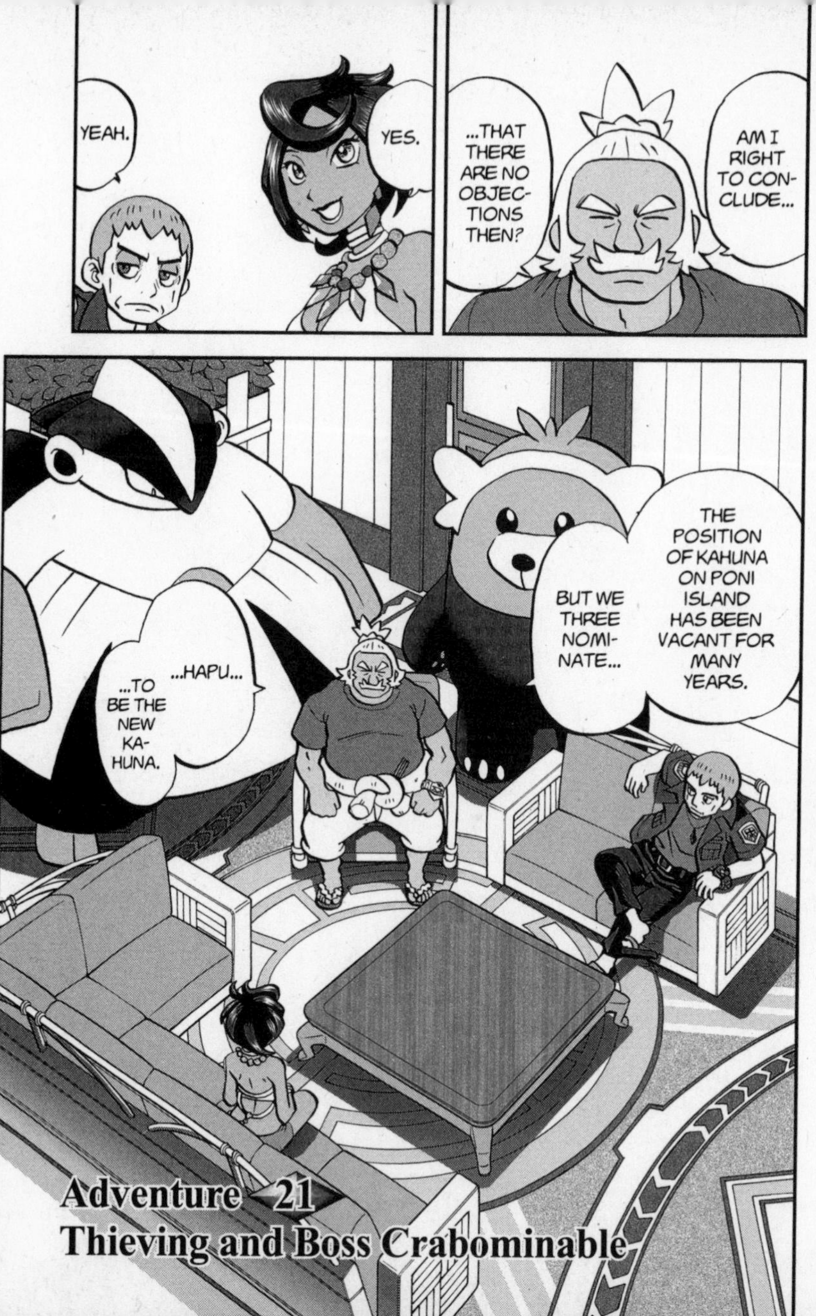
AM I RIGHT TO CON-CLUDE...
...THAT THERE ARE NO OBJEC-TIONS THEN?
YES.
YEAH.
THE POSITION OF KAHUNA ON PONI ISLAND HAS BEEN VACANT FOR MANY YEARS.
BUT WE THREE NOMI-NATE...
...HAPU...
...TO BE THE NEW KA-HUNA.

Adventure 21
Thieving and Boss Crabominable

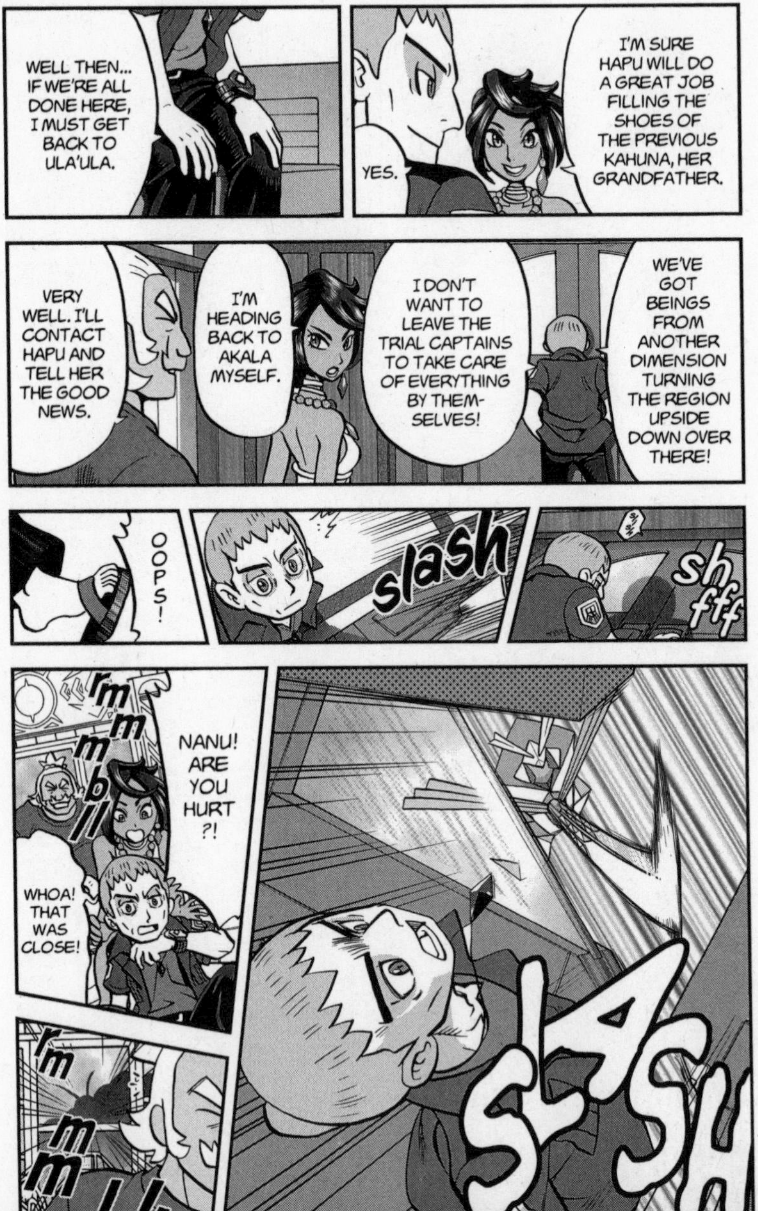
I'M SURE HAPU WILL DO A GREAT JOB FILLING THE SHOES OF THE PREVIOUS KAHUNA, HER GRANDFATHER.
YES.
WELL THEN... IF WE'RE ALL DONE HERE, I MUST GET BACK TO ULA'ULA.
WE'VE GOT BEINGS FROM ANOTHER DIMENSION TURNING THE REGION UPSIDE DOWN OVER THERE!
I DON'T WANT TO LEAVE THE TRIAL CAPTAINS TO TAKE CARE OF EVERYTHING BY THEM-SELVES!
I'M HEADING BACK TO AKALA MYSELF.
VERY WELL. I'LL CONTACT HAPU AND TELL HER THE GOOD NEWS.
shfff
slash
OOPS!
SLASH
rmmmmbl
NANU! ARE YOU HURT?!
WHOA! THAT WAS CLOSE!
rmmmmbl

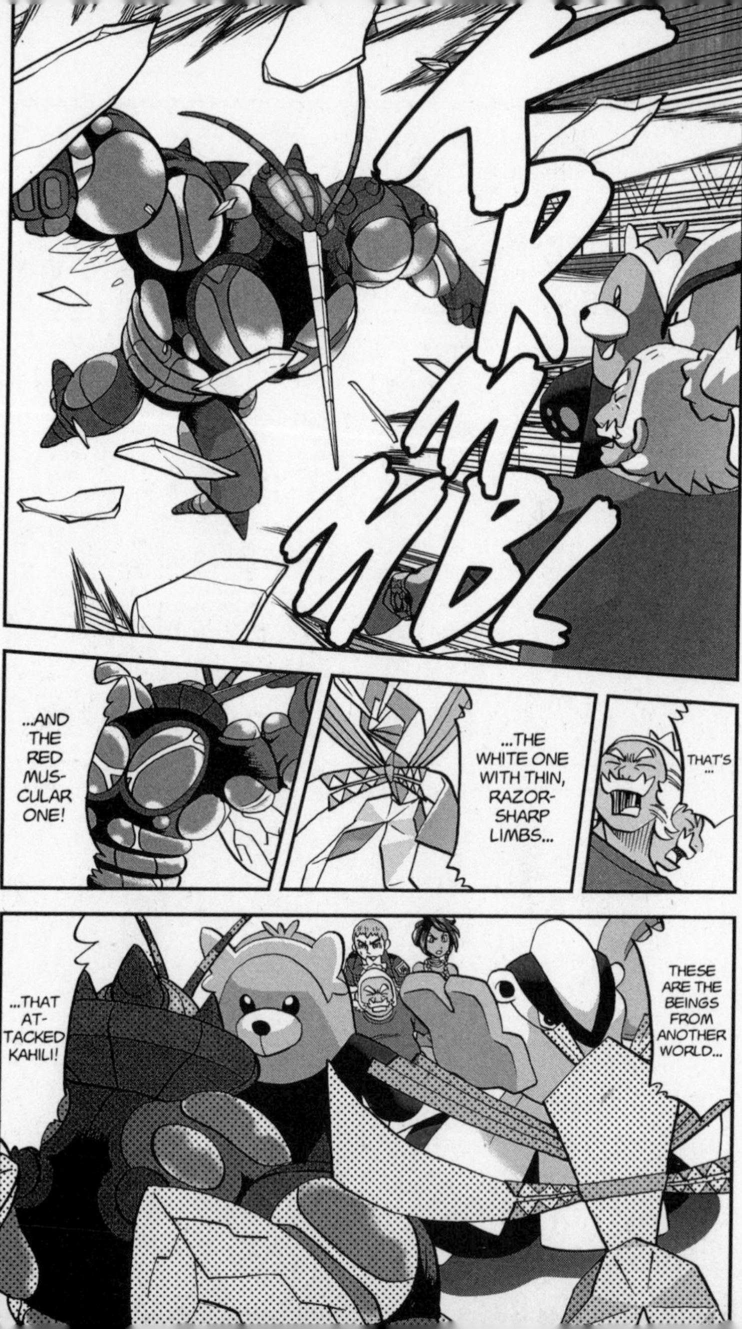
KRMMBL
THAT'S ...
...THE WHITE ONE WITH THIN, RAZOR-SHARP LIMBS...
...AND THE RED MUS-CULAR ONE!
THESE ARE THE BEINGS FROM ANOTHER WORLD...
...THAT AT-TACKED KAHILI!

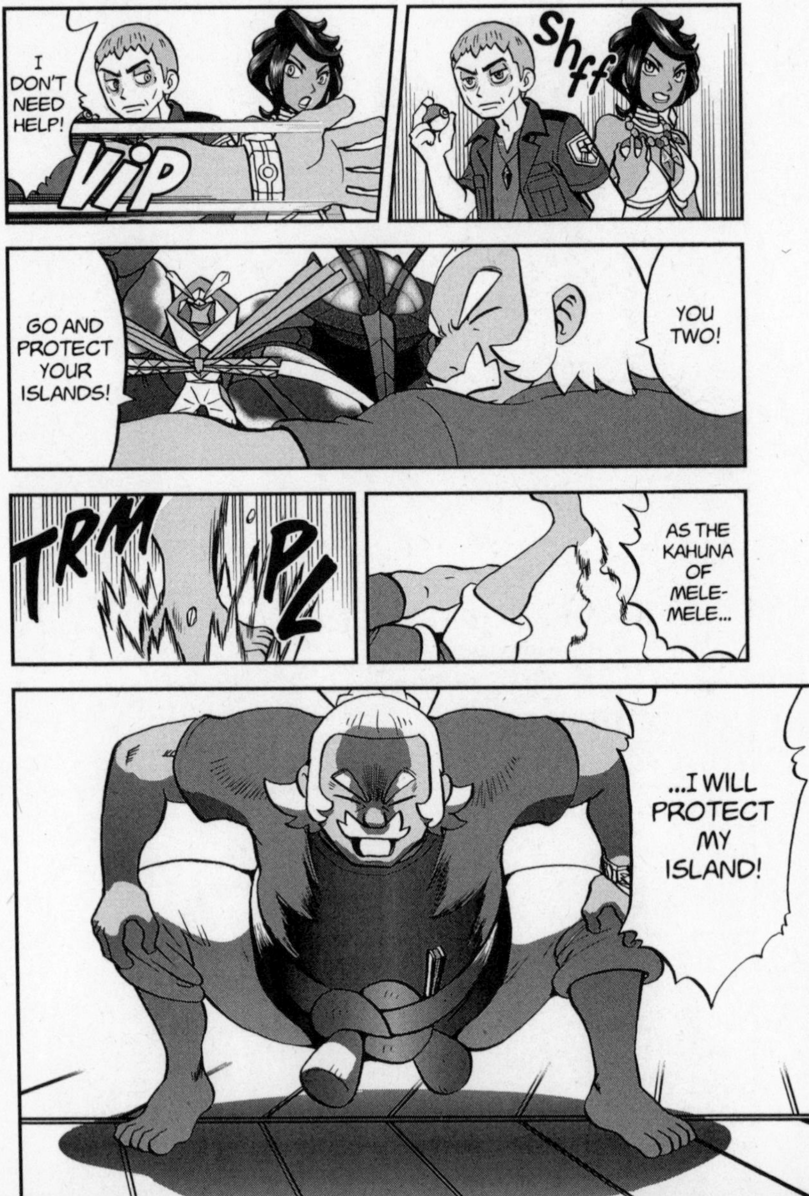
Shff
I DON'T NEED HELP!
ViP
YOU TWO!
GO AND PROTECT YOUR ISLANDS!
AS THE KAHUNA OF MELE-MELE...
TRMPL
...I WILL PROTECT MY ISLAND!

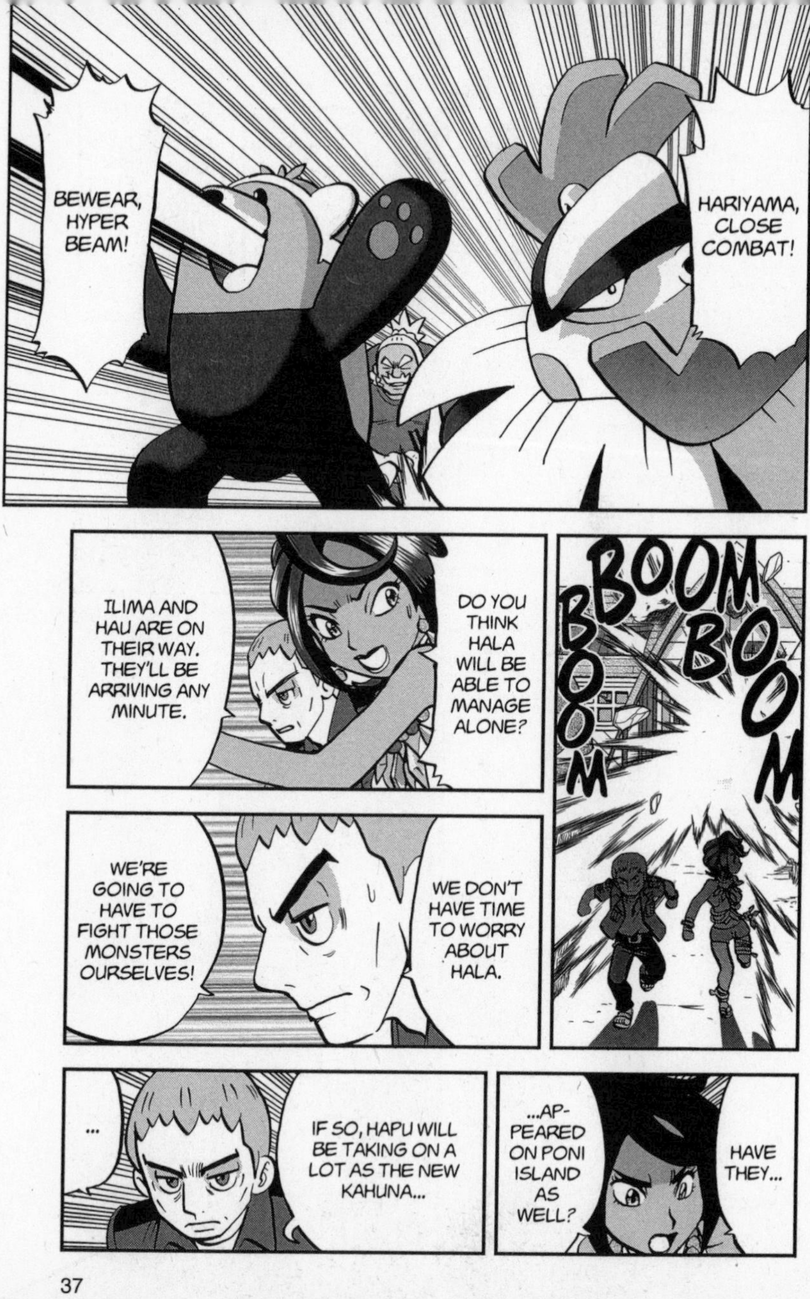
HARIYAMA, CLOSE COMBAT!
BEWEAR, HYPER BEAM!
BOOM
BOOM
BOOM
BOOM
DO YOU THINK HALA WILL BE ABLE TO MANAGE ALONE?
ILIMA AND HAU ARE ON THEIR WAY. THEY'LL BE ARRIVING ANY MINUTE.
WE DON'T HAVE TIME TO WORRY ABOUT HALA.
WE'RE GOING TO HAVE TO FIGHT THOSE MONSTERS OURSELVES!
HAVE THEY...
...AP-PEARED ON PONI ISLAND AS WELL?
IF SO, HAPU WILL BE TAKING ON A LOT AS THE NEW KAHUNA...
...

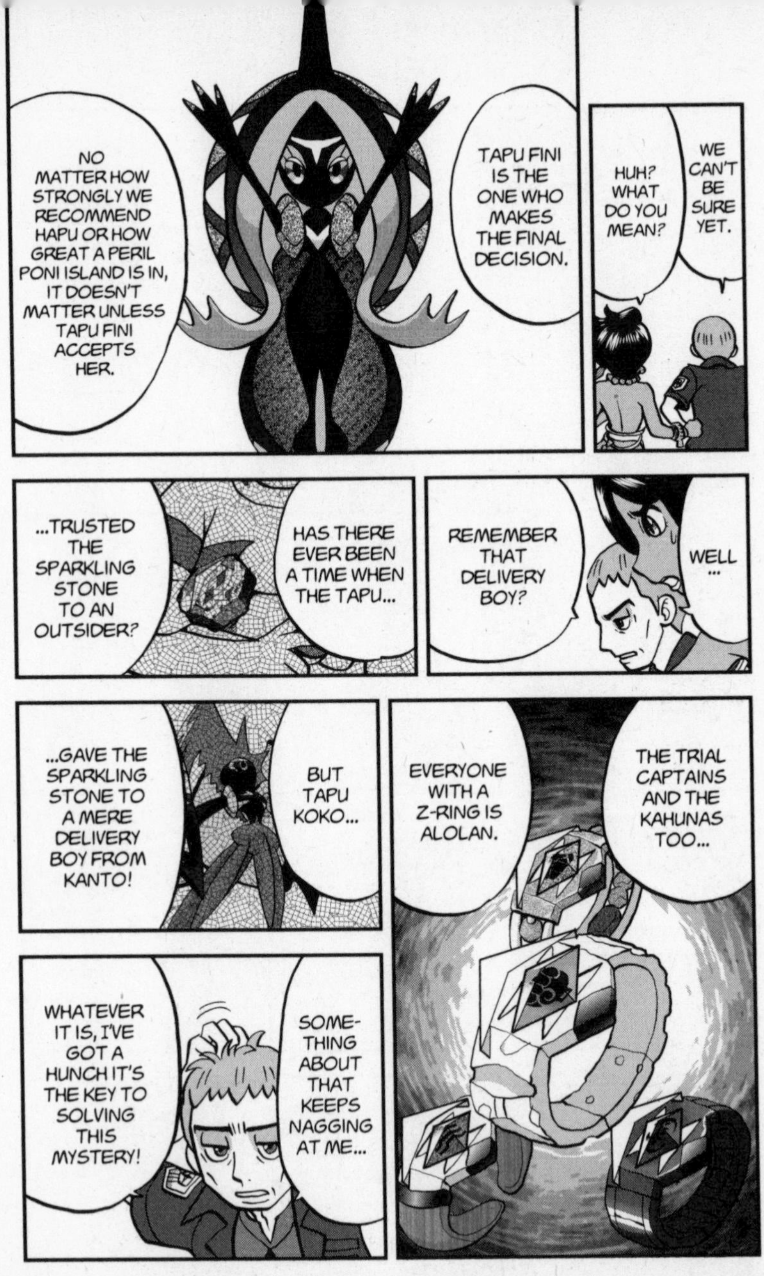
WE CAN'T BE SURE YET.
HUH? WHAT DO YOU MEAN?
TAPU FINI IS THE ONE WHO MAKES THE FINAL DECISION.
NO MATTER HOW STRONGLY WE RECOMMEND HAPU OR HOW GREAT A PERIL PONI ISLAND IS IN, IT DOESN'T MATTER UNLESS TAPU FINI ACCEPTS HER.
WELL...
REMEMBER THAT DELIVERY BOY?
HAS THERE EVER BEEN A TIME WHEN THE TAPU...
...TRUSTED THE SPARKLING STONE TO AN OUTSIDER?
THE TRIAL CAPTAINS AND THE KAHUNAS TOO...
EVERYONE WITH A Z-RING IS ALOLAN.
BUT TAPU KOKO...
...GAVE THE SPARKLING STONE TO A MERE DELIVERY BOY FROM KANTO!
SOME-THING ABOUT THAT KEEPS NAGGING AT ME...
WHATEVER IT IS, I'VE GOT A HUNCH IT'S THE KEY TO SOLVING THIS MYSTERY!

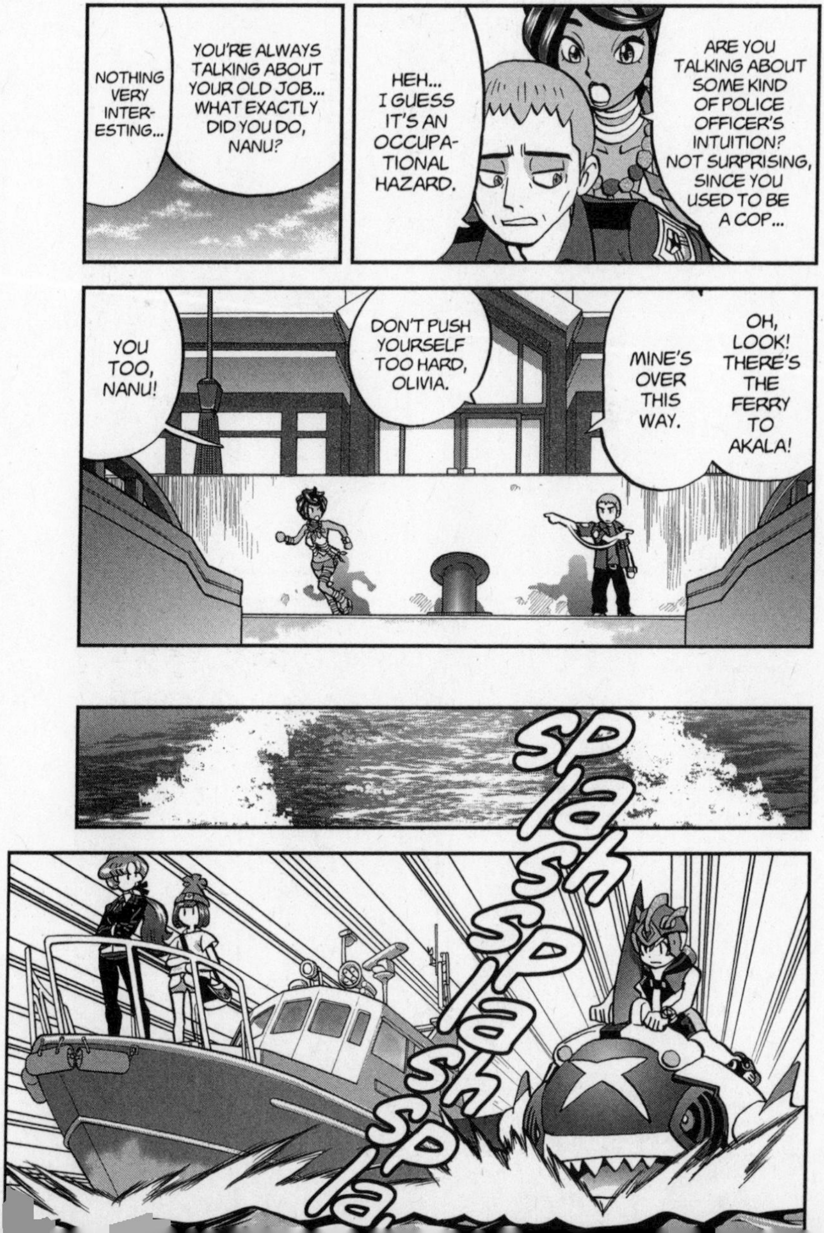
ARE YOU TALKING ABOUT SOME KIND OF POLICE OFFICER'S INTUITION? NOT SURPRISING, SINCE YOU USED TO BE A COP...
HEH... I GUESS IT'S AN OCCUPATIONAL HAZARD.
YOU'RE ALWAYS TALKING ABOUT YOUR OLD JOB... WHAT EXACTLY DID YOU DO, NANU?
NOTHING VERY INTERESTING...
OH, LOOK! THERE'S THE FERRY TO AKALA!
MINE'S OVER THIS WAY.
DON'T PUSH YOURSELF TOO HARD, OLIVIA.
YOU TOO, NANU!
splash
splash
spla

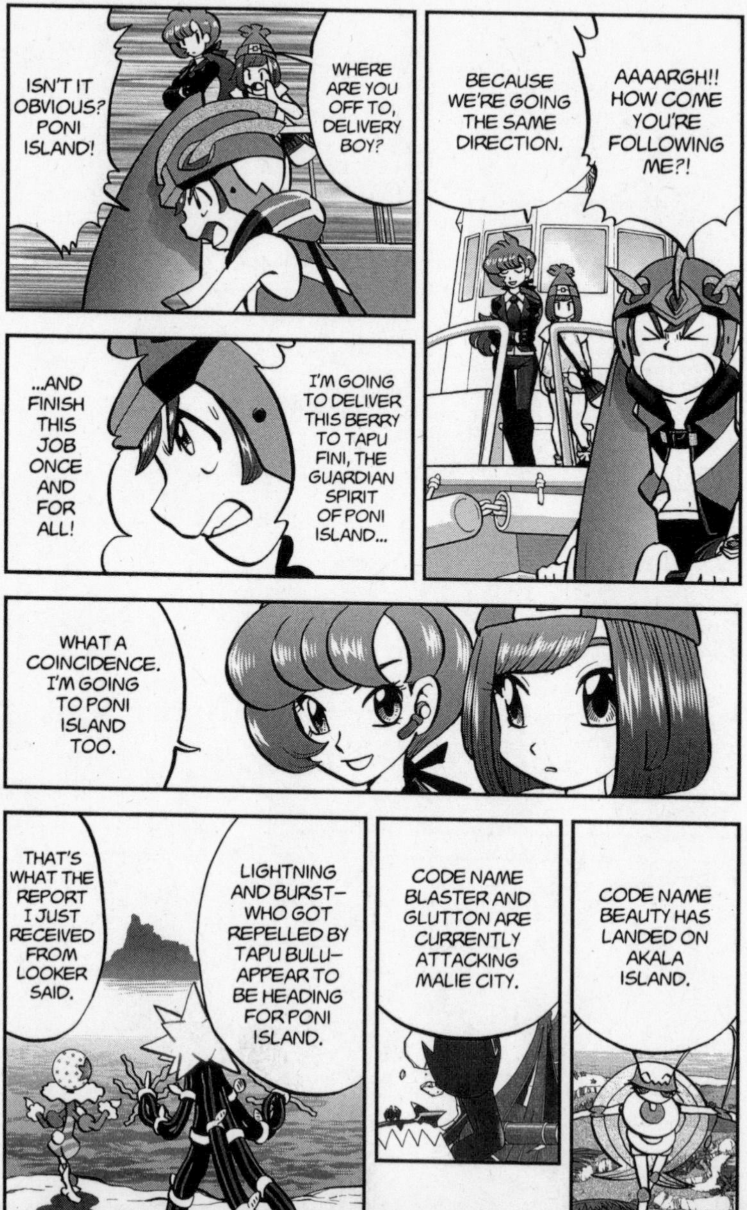
AAAARGH!! HOW COME YOU'RE FOLLOWING ME?!
BECAUSE WE'RE GOING THE SAME DIRECTION.
WHERE ARE YOU OFF TO, DELIVERY BOY?
ISN'T IT OBVIOUS? PONI ISLAND!
I'M GOING TO DELIVER THIS BERRY TO TAPU FINI, THE GUARDIAN SPIRIT OF PONI ISLAND...
...AND FINISH THIS JOB ONCE AND FOR ALL!
WHAT A COINCIDENCE. I'M GOING TO PONI ISLAND TOO.
CODE NAME BEAUTY HAS LANDED ON AKALA ISLAND.
CODE NAME BLASTER AND GLUTTON ARE CURRENTLY ATTACKING MALIE CITY.
LIGHTNING AND BURST—WHO GOT REPELLED BY TAPU BULU—APPEAR TO BE HEADING FOR PONI ISLAND.
THAT'S WHAT THE REPORT I JUST RECEIVED FROM LOOKER SAID.

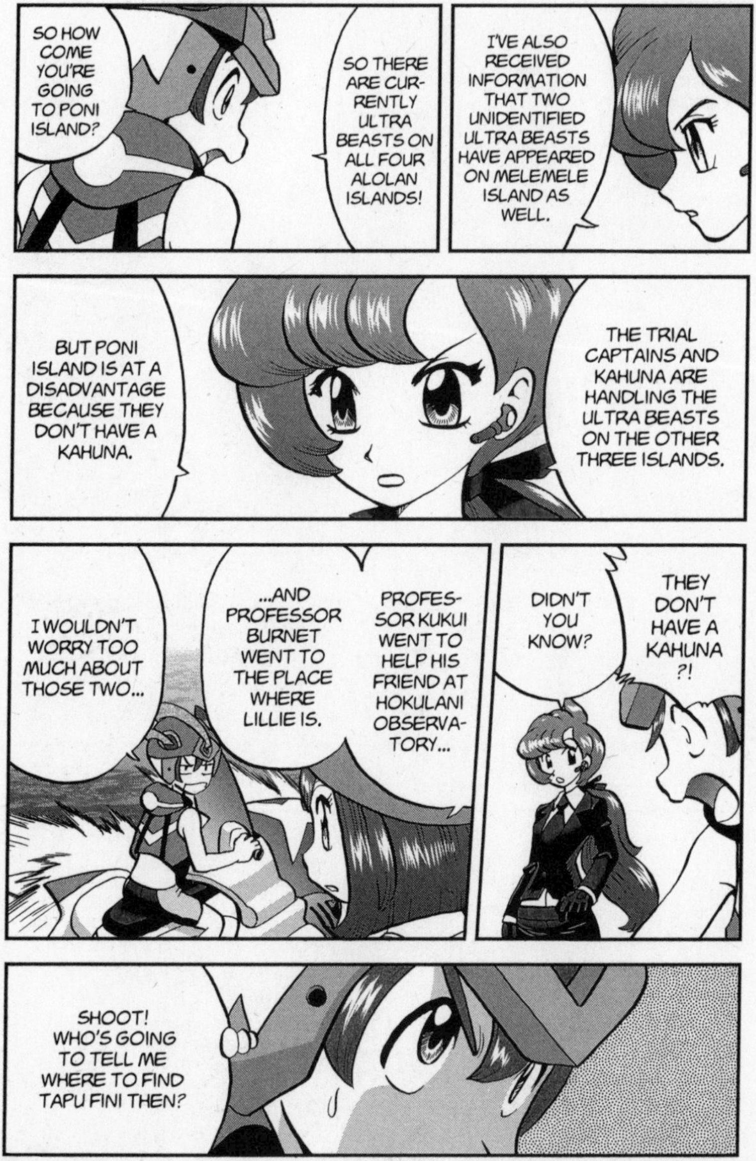
I'VE ALSO RECEIVED INFORMATION THAT TWO UNIDENTIFIED ULTRA BEASTS HAVE APPEARED ON MELEMELE ISLAND AS WELL.
SO THERE ARE CUR-RENTLY ULTRA BEASTS ON ALL FOUR ALOLAN ISLANDS!
SO HOW COME YOU'RE GOING TO PONI ISLAND?
THE TRIAL CAPTAINS AND KAHUNA ARE HANDLING THE ULTRA BEASTS ON THE OTHER THREE ISLANDS.
BUT PONI ISLAND IS AT A DISADVANTAGE BECAUSE THEY DON'T HAVE A KAHUNA.
THEY DON'T HAVE A KAHUNA ?!
DIDN'T YOU KNOW?
PROFES-SOR KUKUI WENT TO HELP HIS FRIEND AT HOKULANI OBSERVA-TORY...
...AND PROFESSOR BURNET WENT TO THE PLACE WHERE LILLIE IS.
I WOULDN'T WORRY TOO MUCH ABOUT THOSE TWO...
SHOOT! WHO'S GOING TO TELL ME WHERE TO FIND TAPU FINI THEN?

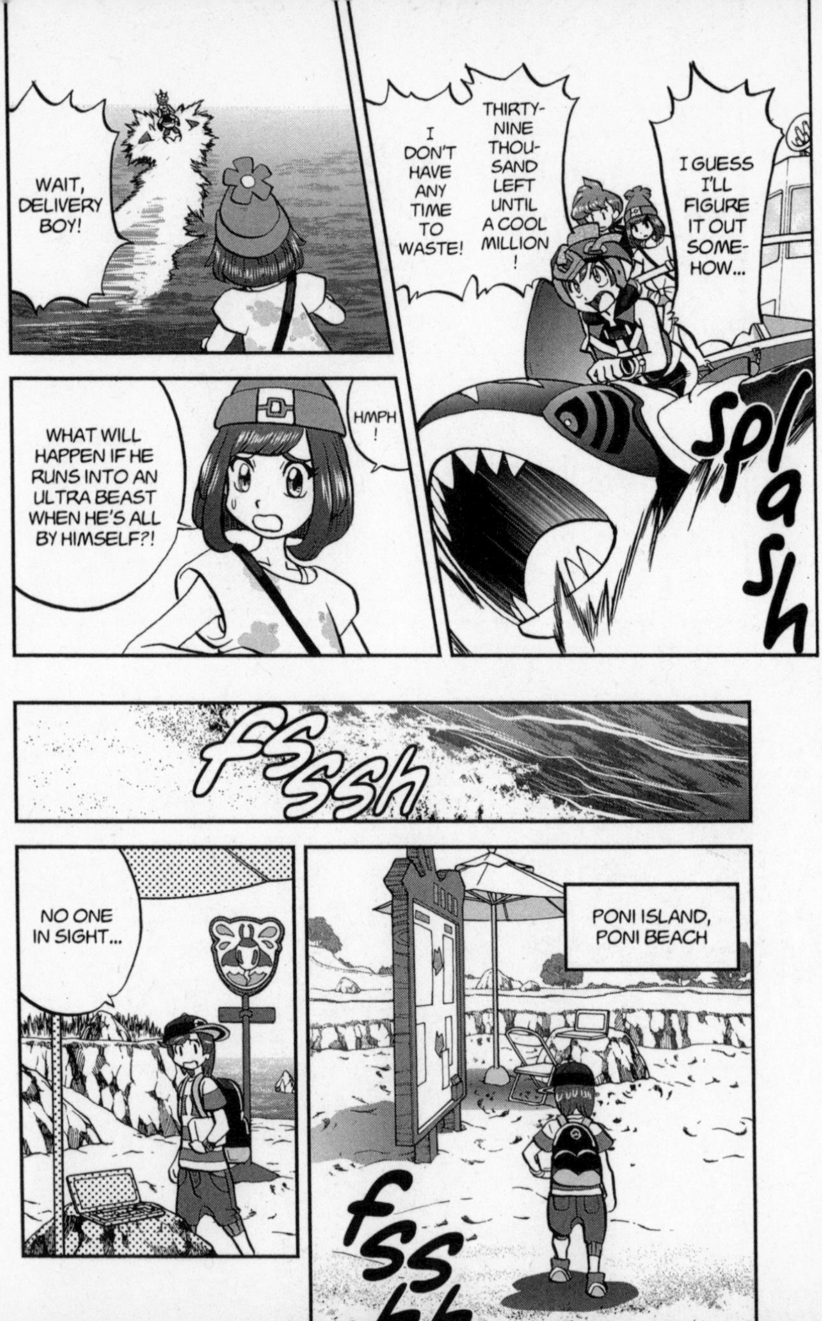
I GUESS I'LL FIGURE IT OUT SOME-HOW...
THIRTY-NINE THOU-SAND LEFT UNTIL A COOL MILLION!
I DON'T HAVE ANY TIME TO WASTE!
splash
WAIT, DELIVERY BOY!
HMPH!
WHAT WILL HAPPEN IF HE RUNS INTO AN ULTRA BEAST WHEN HE'S ALL BY HIMSELF?!
fsssh
PONI ISLAND, PONI BEACH
fss
NO ONE IN SIGHT...

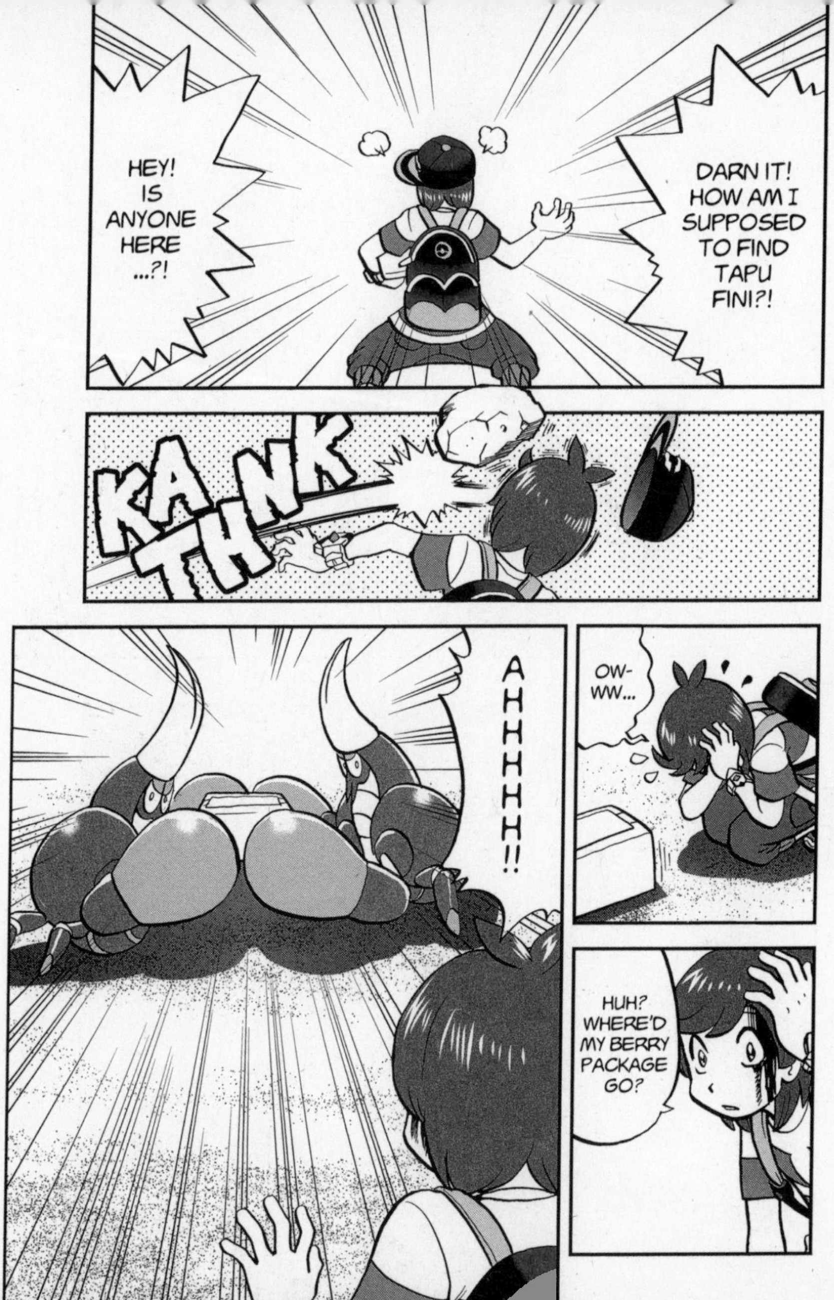
DARN IT! HOW AM I SUPPOSED TO FIND TAPU FINI?!
HEY! IS ANYONE HERE ...?!
KANK TH
OW-WW...
HUH? WHERE'D MY BERRY PACKAGE GO?
AHHHHHH!!

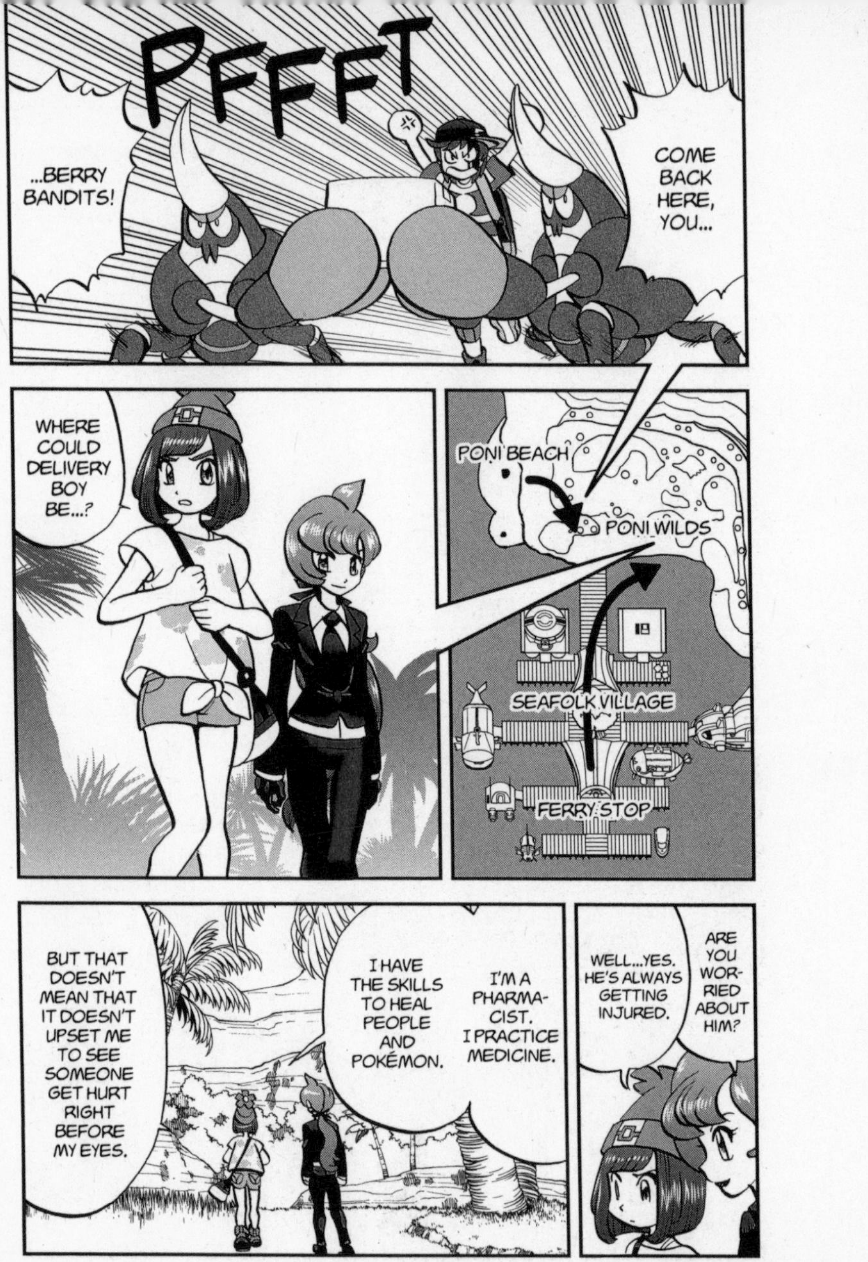
PFFFT
COME BACK HERE, YOU...
...BERRY BANDITS!
PONI BEACH
PONI WILDS
SEAFOLK VILLAGE
FERRY STOP
WHERE COULD DELIVERY BOY BE...?
ARE YOU WORRIED ABOUT HIM?
WELL...YES. HE'S ALWAYS GETTING INJURED.
I'M A PHARMACIST. I PRACTICE MEDICINE.
I HAVE THE SKILLS TO HEAL PEOPLE AND POKÉMON.
BUT THAT DOESN'T MEAN THAT IT DOESN'T UPSET ME TO SEE SOMEONE GET HURT RIGHT BEFORE MY EYES.

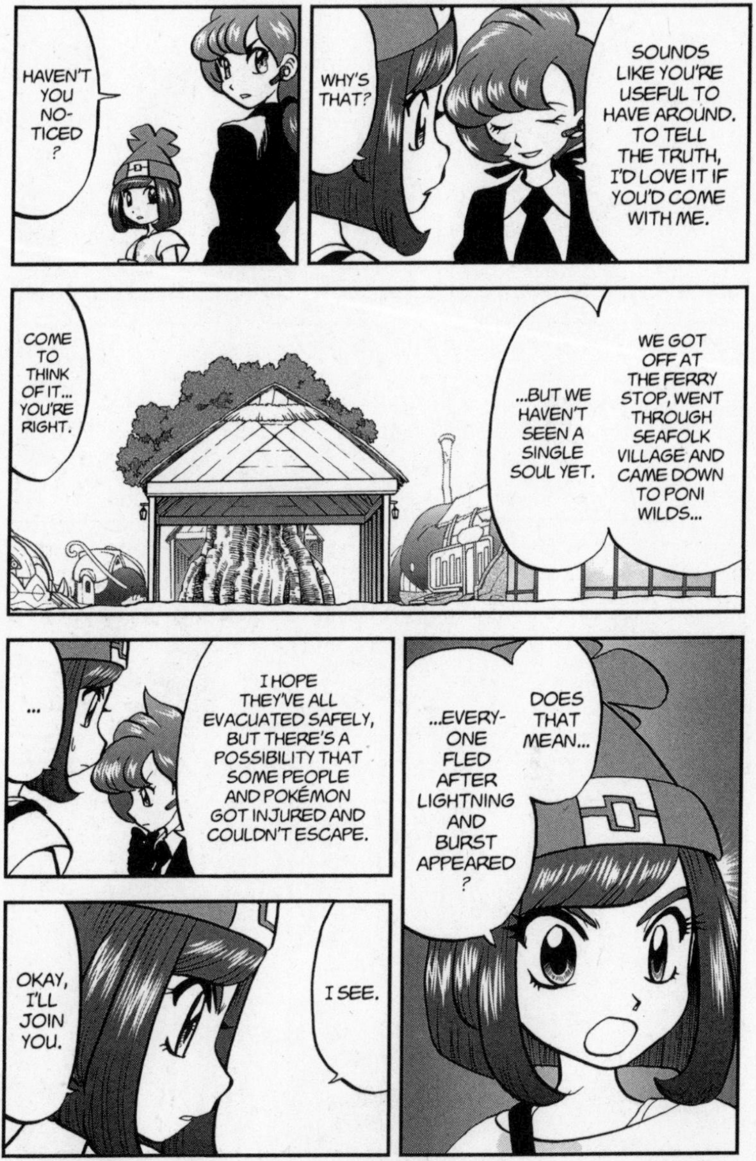

SOUNDS LIKE YOU'RE USEFUL TO HAVE AROUND. TO TELL THE TRUTH, I'D LOVE IT IF YOU'D COME WITH ME.
WHY'S THAT?
HAVEN'T YOU NO-TICED?
WE GOT OFF AT THE FERRY STOP, WENT THROUGH SEAFOLK VILLAGE AND CAME DOWN TO PONI WILDS...
...BUT WE HAVEN'T SEEN A SINGLE SOUL YET.
COME TO THINK OF IT... YOU'RE RIGHT.
DOES THAT MEAN...
...EVERY-ONE FLED AFTER LIGHTNING AND BURST APPEARED?
I HOPE THEY'VE ALL EVACUATED SAFELY, BUT THERE'S A POSSIBILITY THAT SOME PEOPLE AND POKÉMON GOT INJURED AND COULDN'T ESCAPE.
...
I SEE.
OKAY, I'LL JOIN YOU.

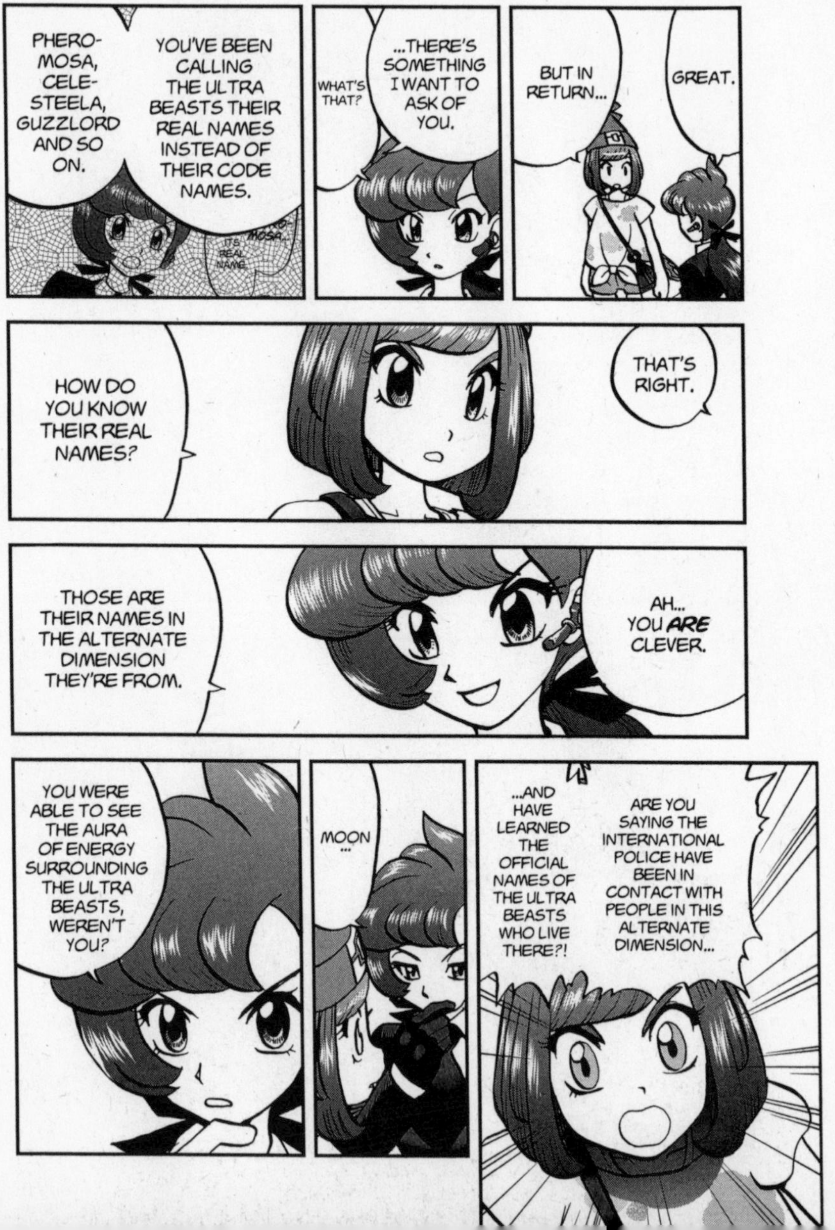
GREAT.
BUT IN RETURN...
...THERE'S SOMETHING I WANT TO ASK OF YOU.
WHAT'S THAT?
YOU'VE BEEN CALLING THE ULTRA BEASTS THEIR REAL NAMES INSTEAD OF THEIR CODE NAMES.
ITS REAL NAME
PHERO-MOSA, CELE-STEELA, GUZZLORD AND SO ON.
THAT'S RIGHT.
HOW DO YOU KNOW THEIR REAL NAMES?
AH... YOU **ARE** CLEVER.
THOSE ARE THEIR NAMES IN THE ALTERNATE DIMENSION THEY'RE FROM.
ARE YOU SAYING THE INTERNATIONAL POLICE HAVE BEEN IN CONTACT WITH PEOPLE IN THIS ALTERNATE DIMENSION...
...AND HAVE LEARNED THE OFFICIAL NAMES OF THE ULTRA BEASTS WHO LIVE THERE?!
MOON...
YOU WERE ABLE TO SEE THE AURA OF ENERGY SURROUNDING THE ULTRA BEASTS, WEREN'T YOU?

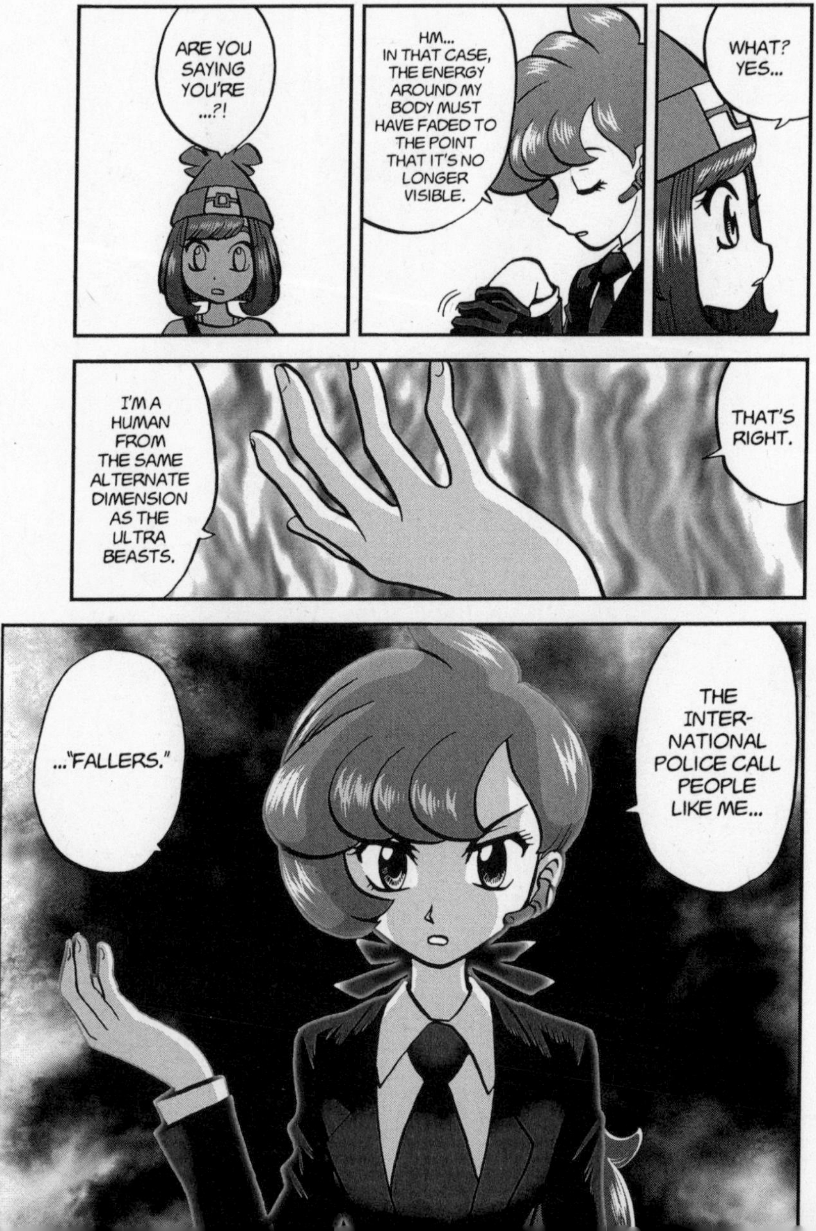
WHAT? YES...
HM... IN THAT CASE, THE ENERGY AROUND MY BODY MUST HAVE FADED TO THE POINT THAT IT'S NO LONGER VISIBLE.
ARE YOU SAYING YOU'RE ...?!
THAT'S RIGHT.
I'M A HUMAN FROM THE SAME ALTERNATE DIMENSION AS THE ULTRA BEASTS.
THE INTER-NATIONAL POLICE CALL PEOPLE LIKE ME...
..."FALLERS."

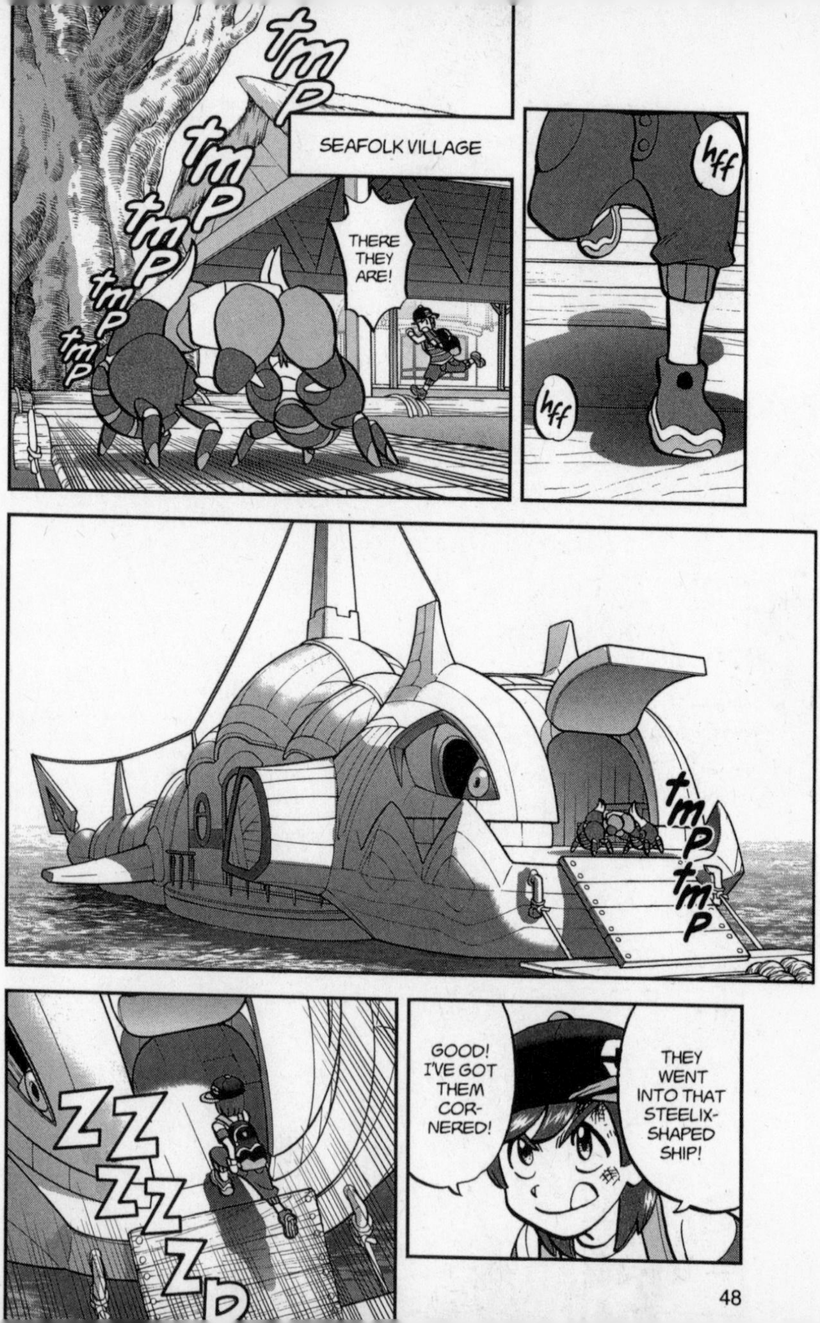
hff
hff
SEAFOLK VILLAGE
tmp tmp tmp tmp tmp tmp
THERE THEY ARE!
tmp tmp tmp
THEY WENT INTO THAT STEELIX-SHAPED SHIP!
GOOD! I'VE GOT THEM COR-NERED!
ZZZZZp

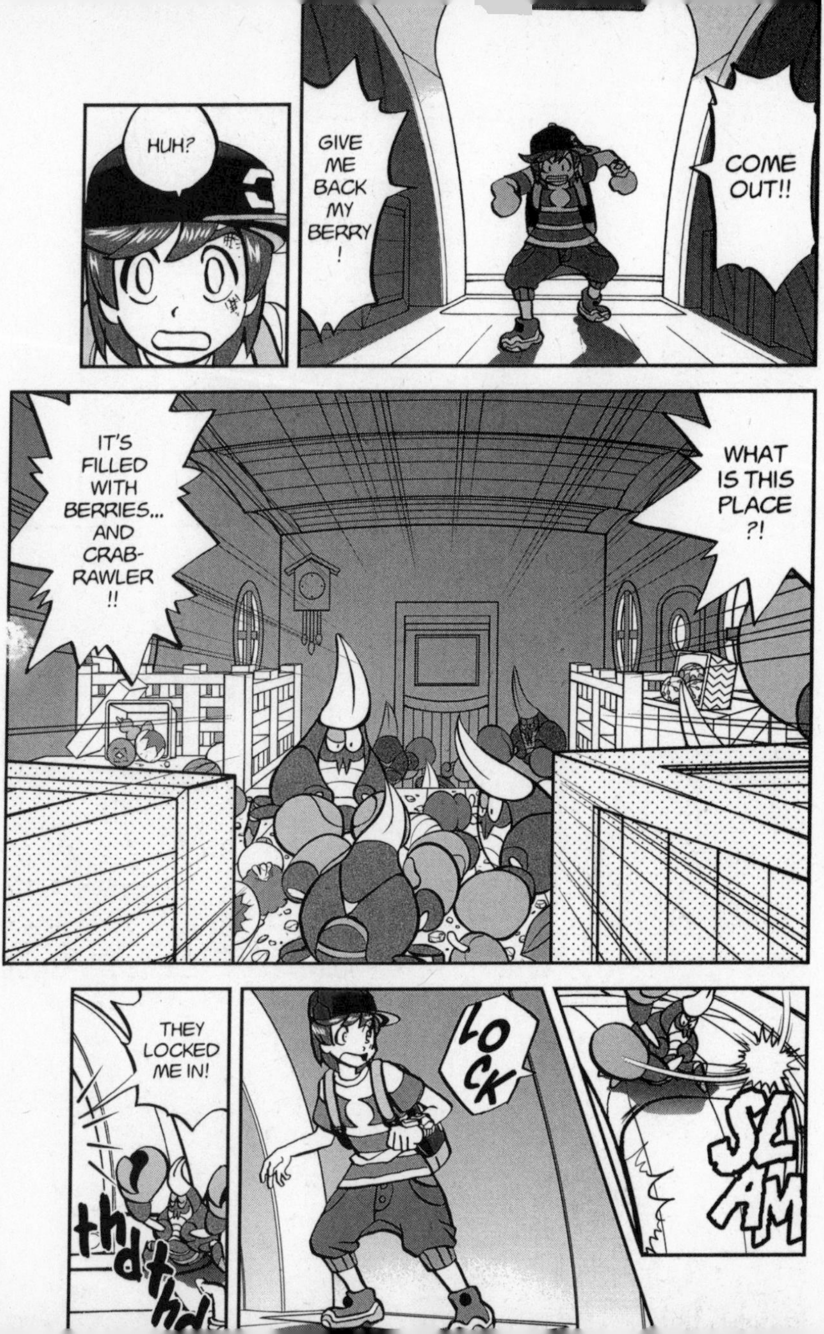

COME OUT!!
GIVE ME BACK MY BERRY!
HUH?
WHAT IS THIS PLACE?!
IT'S FILLED WITH BERRIES... AND CRAB-RAWLER!!
SLAM
LOCK
THEY LOCKED ME IN!
thd thd thd

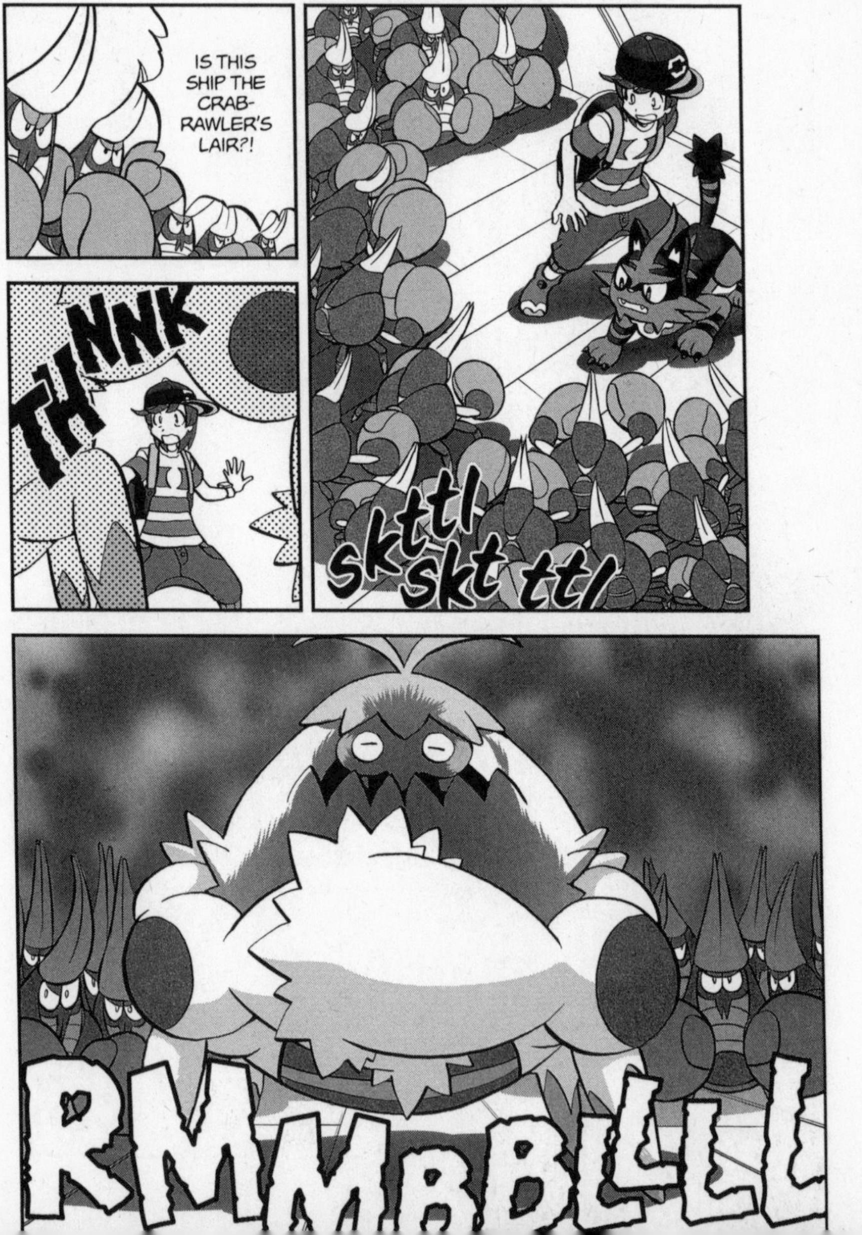
skttl
skt ttl
IS THIS SHIP THE CRAB-RAWLER'S LAIR?!
THNNK
RMMBLLL

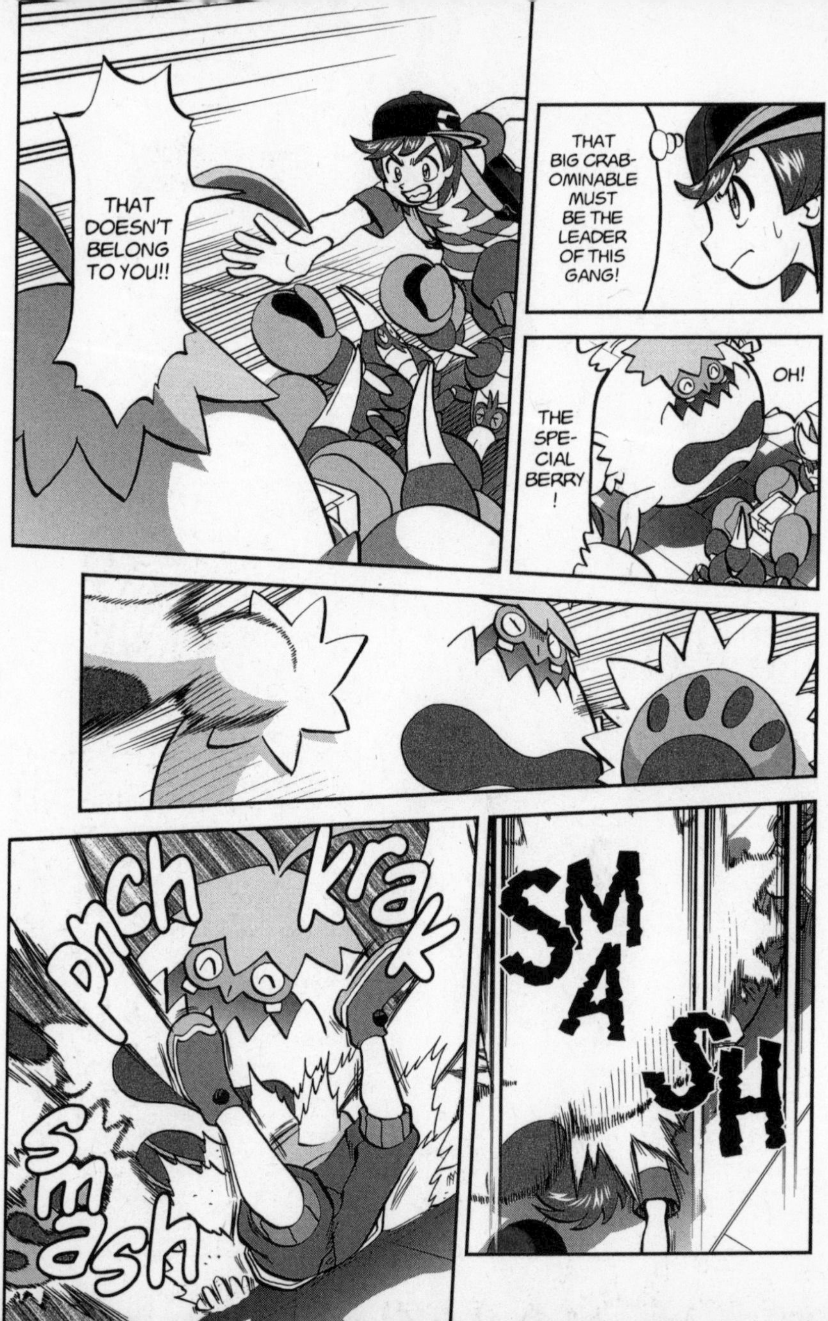
THAT BIG CRAB-OMINABLE MUST BE THE LEADER OF THIS GANG!
OH!
THE SPE-CIAL BERRY!
THAT DOESN'T BELONG TO YOU!!
SMASH
pnch
krak
smash

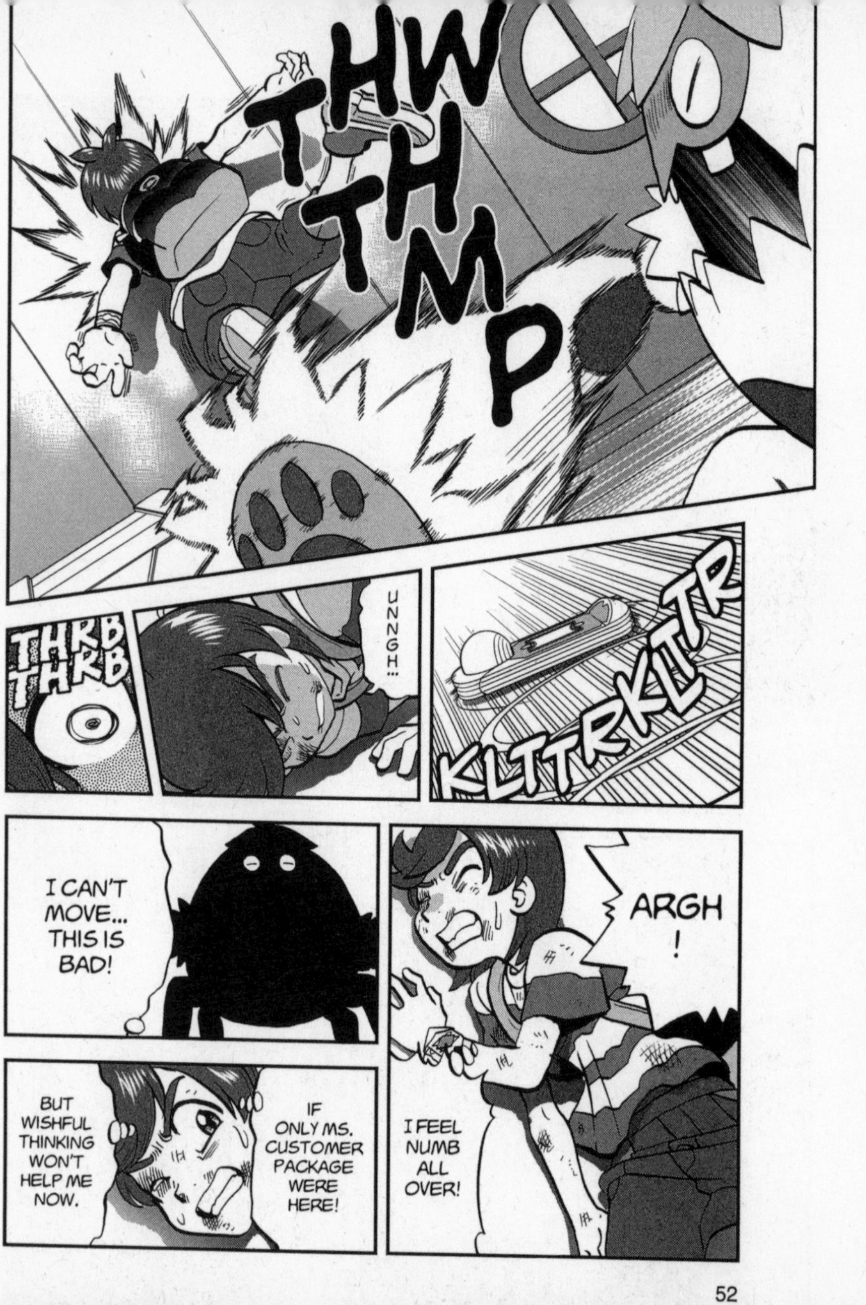

THWTHMP
KLTTRKLTTR
UNNGH!!
THRB THRB
ARGH!
I FEEL NUMB ALL OVER!
I CAN'T MOVE... THIS IS BAD!
IF ONLY MS. CUSTOMER PACKAGE WERE HERE!
BUT WISHFUL THINKING WON'T HELP ME NOW.

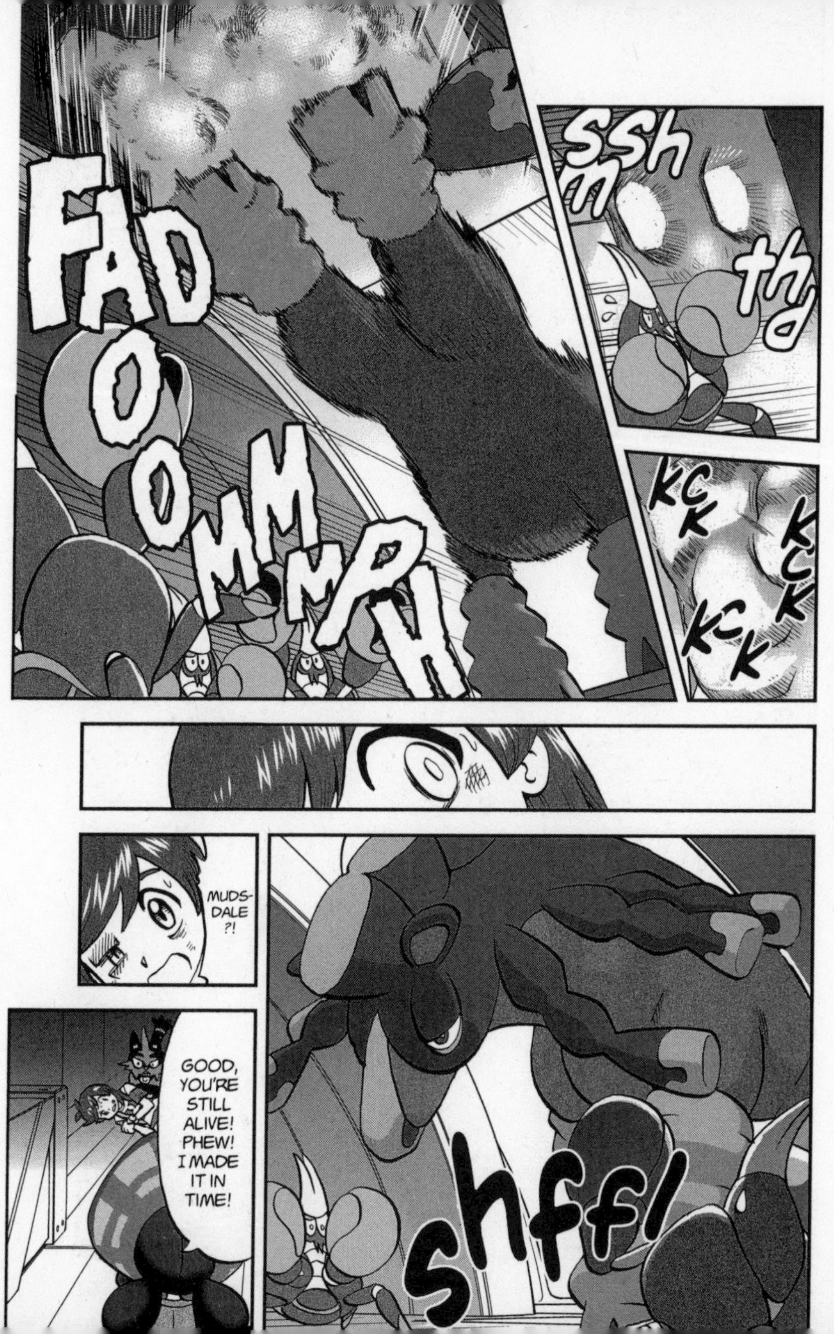
sshmooth
KCK
KCK
KCK
FADOOMMPH
shff!
MUDSDALE?!
GOOD, YOU'RE STILL ALIVE! PHEW! I MADE IT IN TIME!

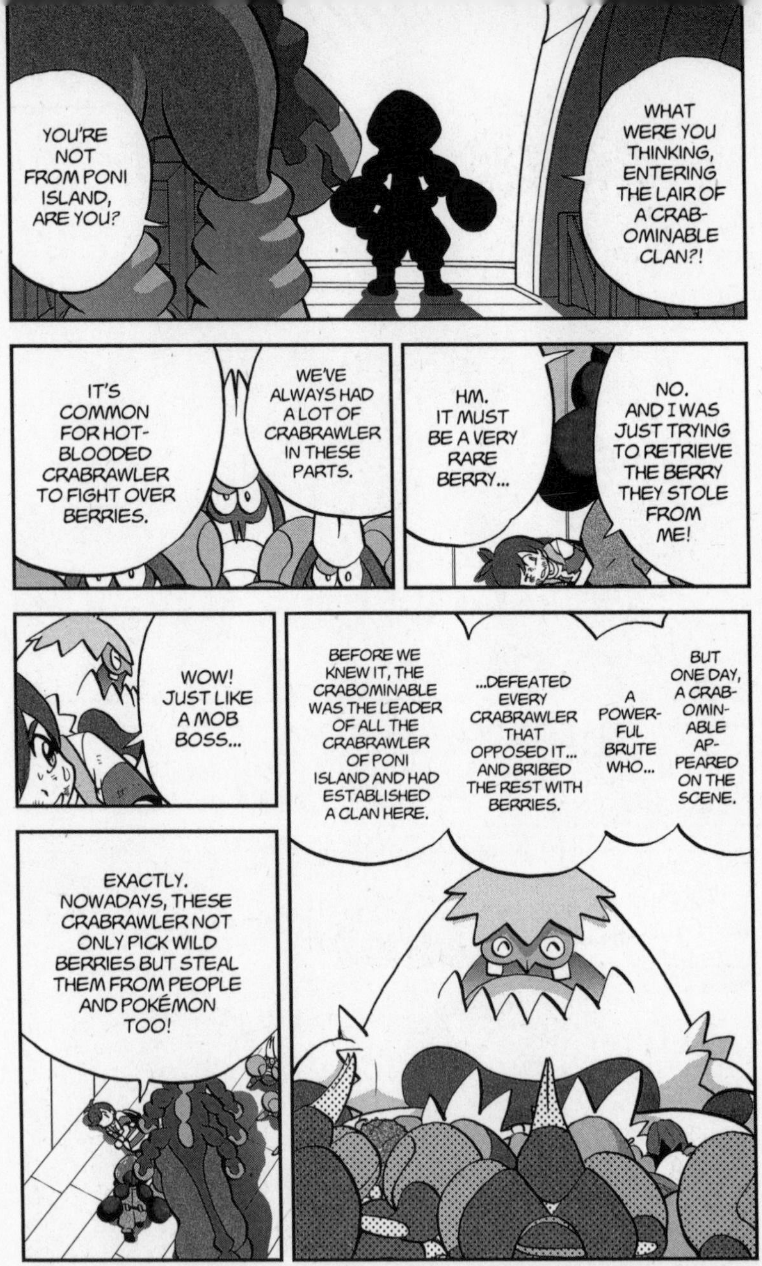
WHAT WERE YOU THINKING, ENTERING THE LAIR OF A CRAB-OMINABLE CLAN?!
YOU'RE NOT FROM PONI ISLAND, ARE YOU?
NO. AND I WAS JUST TRYING TO RETRIEVE THE BERRY THEY STOLE FROM ME!
HM. IT MUST BE A VERY RARE BERRY...
WE'VE ALWAYS HAD A LOT OF CRABRAWLER IN THESE PARTS.
IT'S COMMON FOR HOT-BLOODED CRABRAWLER TO FIGHT OVER BERRIES.
BUT ONE DAY, A CRAB-OMIN-ABLE AP-PEARED ON THE SCENE.
A POWER-FUL BRUTE WHO...
...DEFEATED EVERY CRABRAWLER THAT OPPOSED IT... AND BRIBED THE REST WITH BERRIES.
BEFORE WE KNEW IT, THE CRABOMINABLE WAS THE LEADER OF ALL THE CRABRAWLER OF PONI ISLAND AND HAD ESTABLISHED A CLAN HERE.
WOW! JUST LIKE A MOB BOSS...
EXACTLY. NOWADAYS, THESE CRABRAWLER NOT ONLY PICK WILD BERRIES BUT STEAL THEM FROM PEOPLE AND POKÉMON TOO!

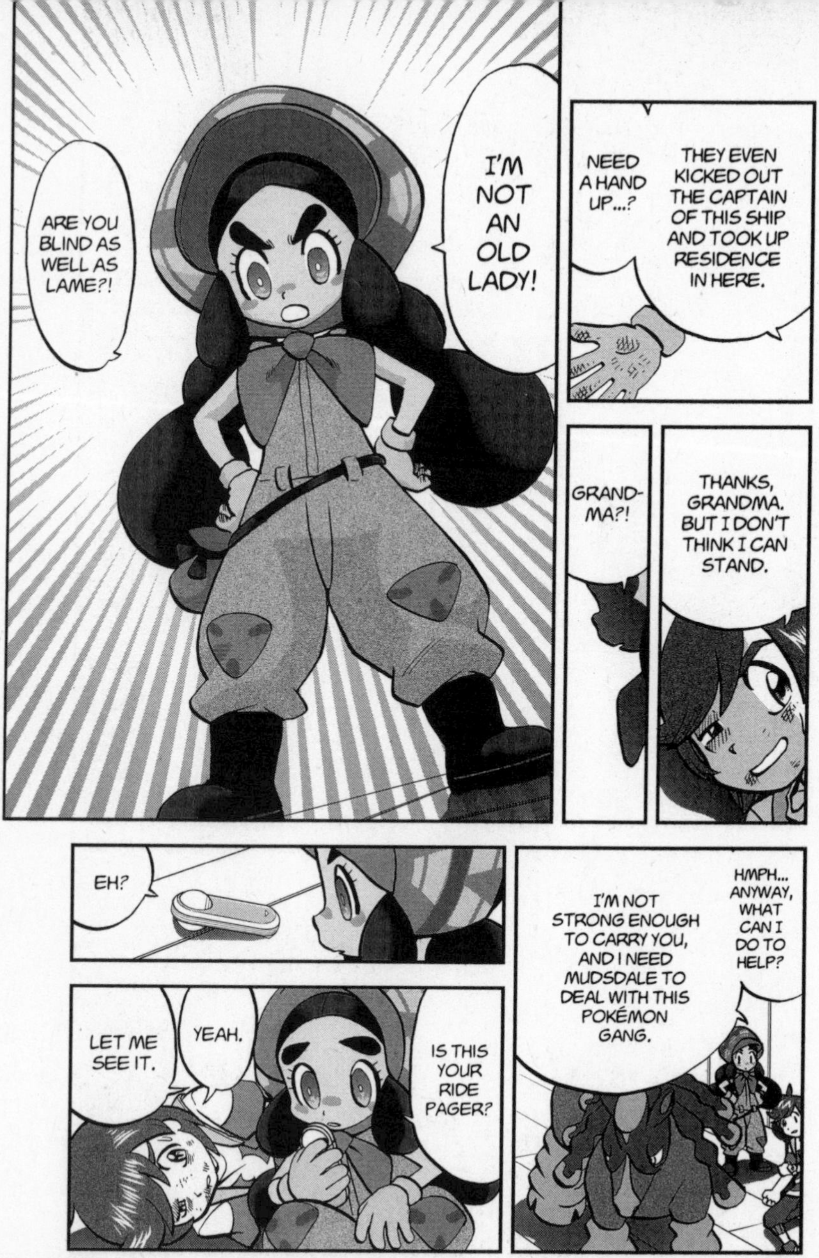
THEY EVEN KICKED OUT THE CAPTAIN OF THIS SHIP AND TOOK UP RESIDENCE IN HERE.
NEED A HAND UP...?
THANKS, GRANDMA. BUT I DON'T THINK I CAN STAND.
GRAND-MA?!
I'M NOT AN OLD LADY!
ARE YOU BLIND AS WELL AS LAME?!
HMPH... ANYWAY, WHAT CAN I DO TO HELP?
I'M NOT STRONG ENOUGH TO CARRY YOU, AND I NEED MUDSDALE TO DEAL WITH THIS POKÉMON GANG.
EH?
IS THIS YOUR RIDE PAGER?
YEAH.
LET ME SEE IT.

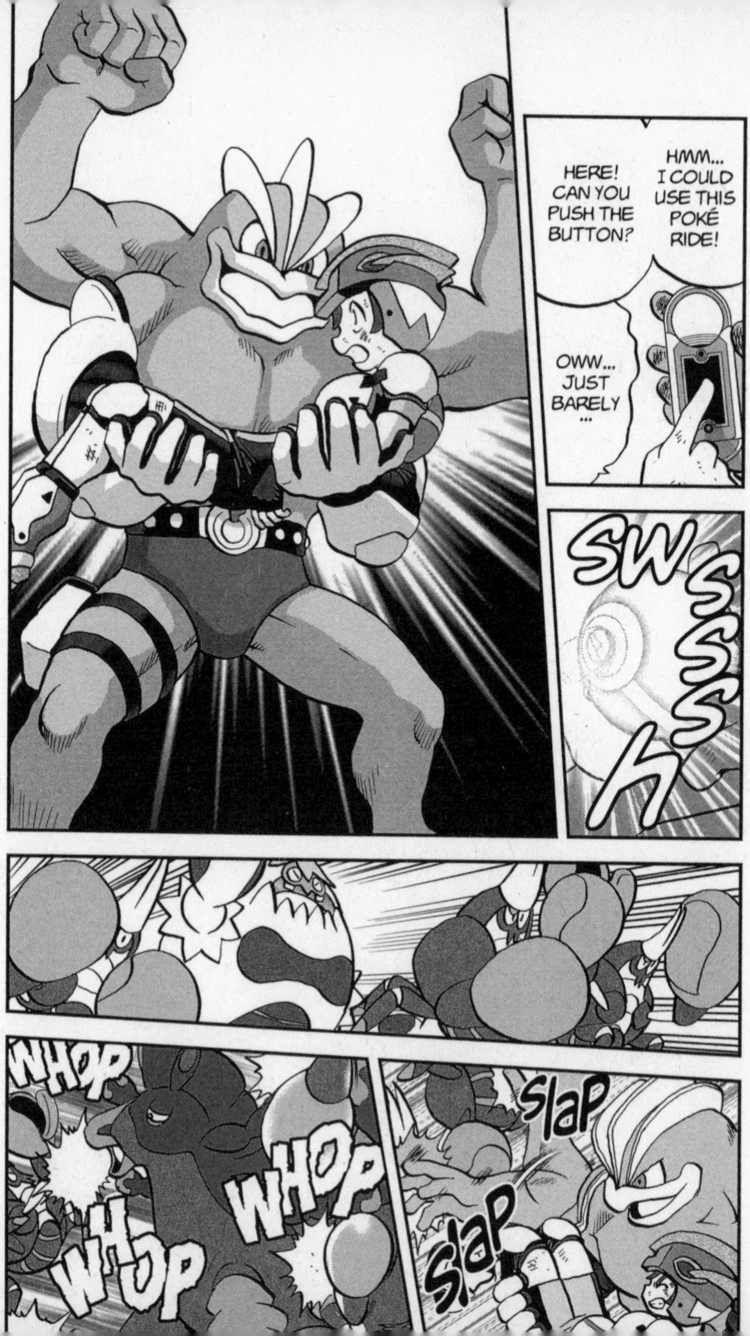
HMM... I COULD USE THIS POKÉ RIDE!
HERE! CAN YOU PUSH THE BUTTON?
OWW... JUST BARELY ...
SWSSSSH
SLAP
SLAP
WHOP
WHOP
WHOP
WHOP

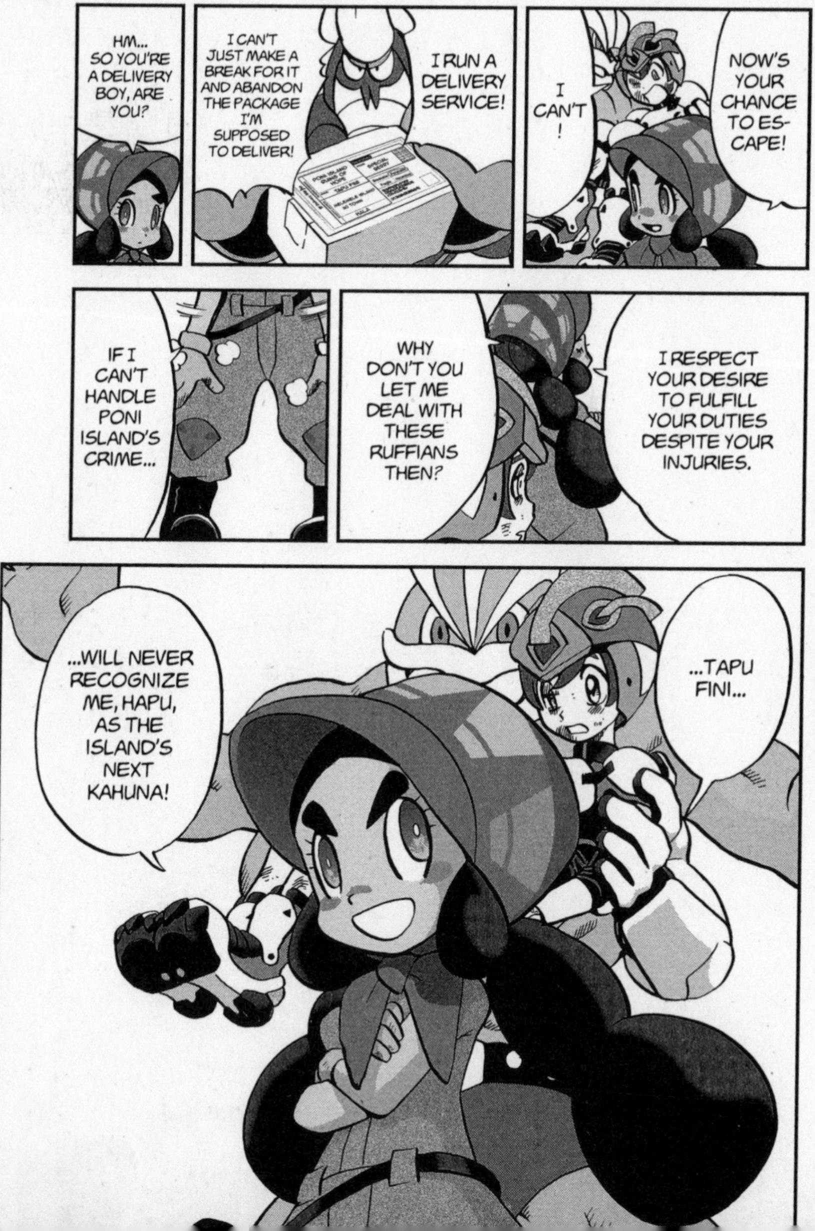
NOW'S YOUR CHANCE TO ES-CAPE!
I CAN'T!
I RUN A DELIVERY SERVICE!
I CAN'T JUST MAKE A BREAK FOR IT AND ABANDON THE PACKAGE I'M SUPPOSED TO DELIVER!
HM... SO YOU'RE A DELIVERY BOY, ARE YOU?
I RESPECT YOUR DESIRE TO FULFILL YOUR DUTIES DESPITE YOUR INJURIES.
WHY DON'T YOU LET ME DEAL WITH THESE RUFFIANS THEN?
IF I CAN'T HANDLE PONI ISLAND'S CRIME...
...TAPU FINI...
...WILL NEVER RECOGNIZE ME, HAPU, AS THE ISLAND'S NEXT KAHUNA!

Aether Paradise

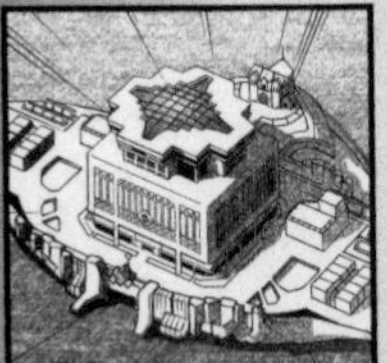

The Aether Foundation is an organization that provides shelter for Pokémon in need. Aether Paradise is an artificial island equipped with modern facilities for housing and caring for Pokémon. Every Alolan has heard their catchy ad jingle by now. ♪

Guide to Alola 18

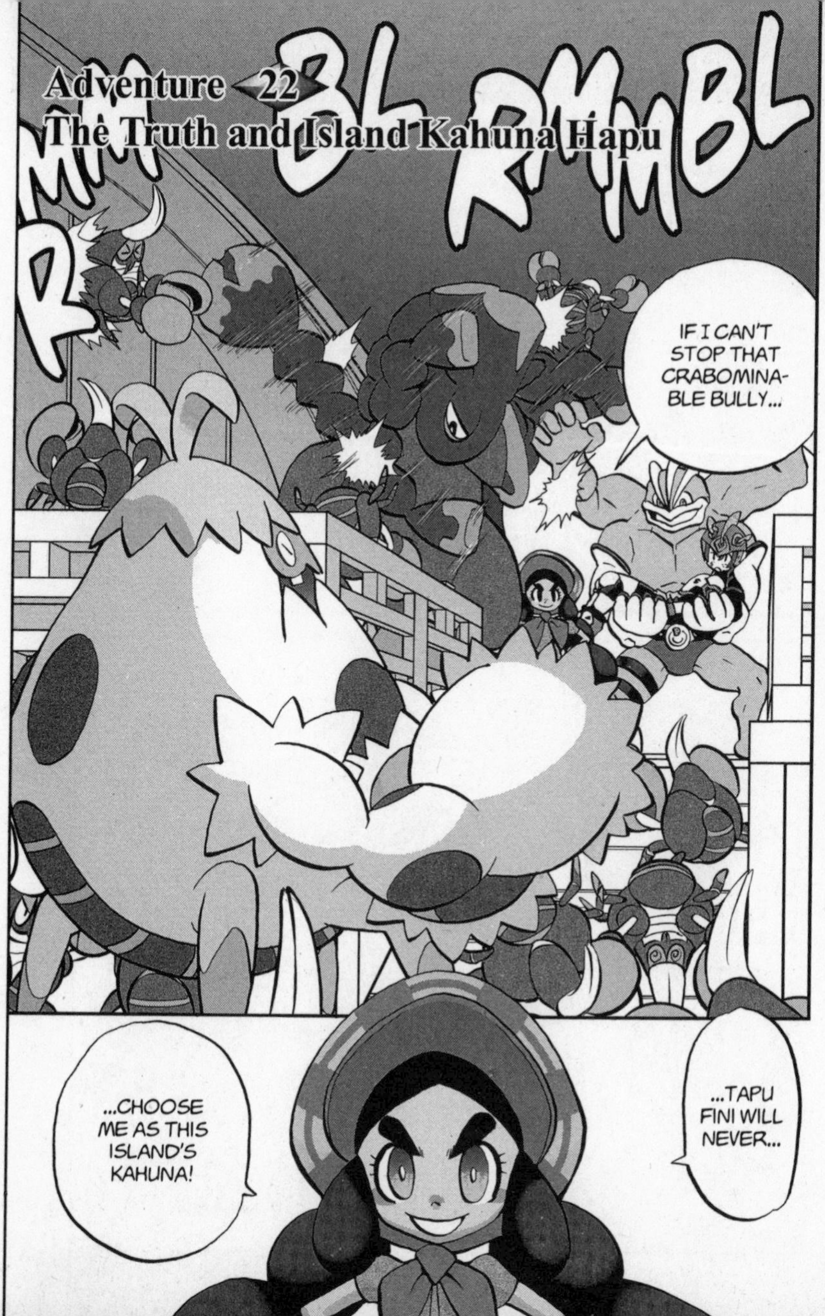
Adventure 22
The Truth and Island Kahuna Hapu
RMMBL
RMMBL
IF I CAN'T STOP THAT CRABOMINA-BLE BULLY...
...TAPU FINI WILL NEVER...
...CHOOSE ME AS THIS ISLAND'S KAHUNA!

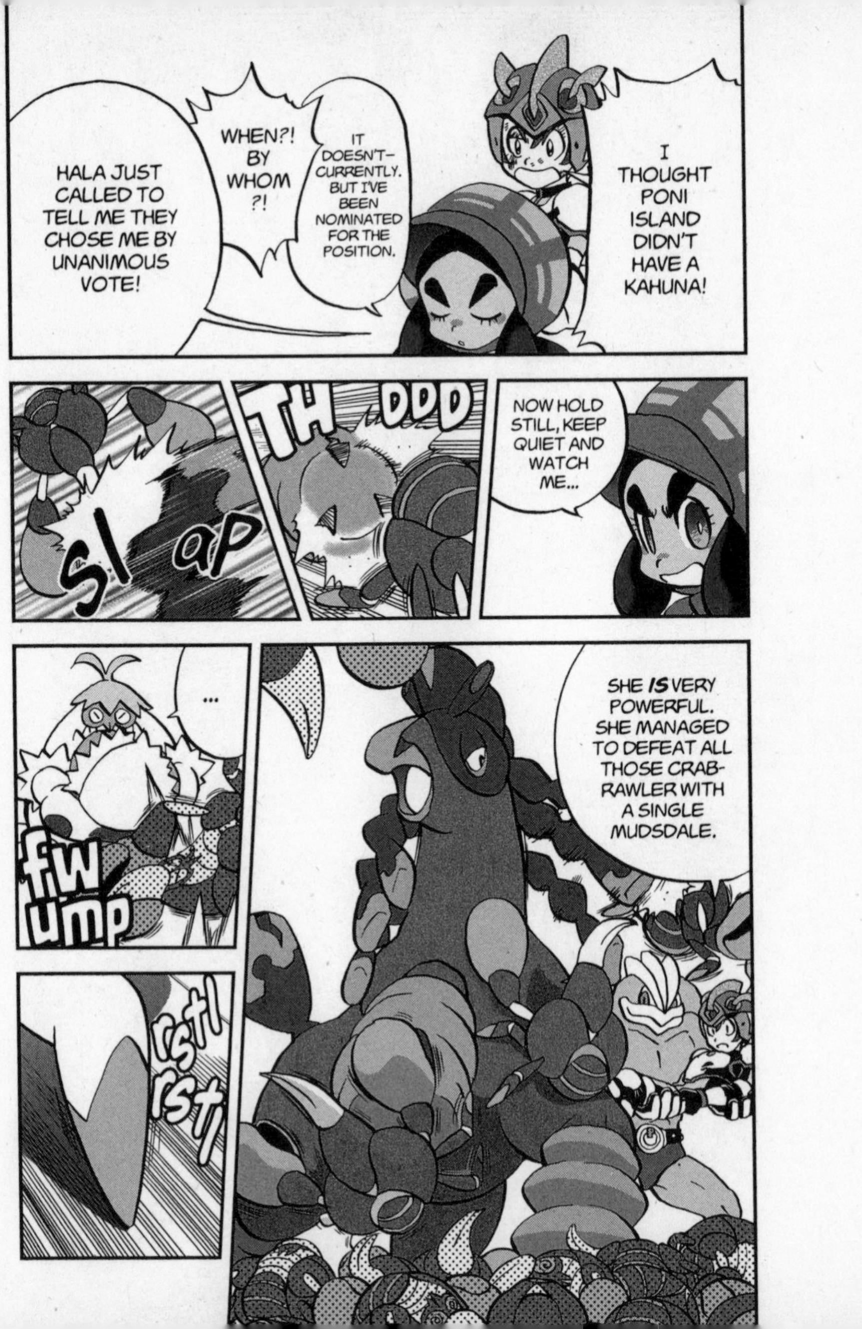
I THOUGHT PONI ISLAND DIDN'T HAVE A KAHUNA!
IT DOESN'T— CURRENTLY. BUT I'VE BEEN NOMINATED FOR THE POSITION.
WHEN?! BY WHOM ?!
HALA JUST CALLED TO TELL ME THEY CHOSE ME BY UNANIMOUS VOTE!
NOW HOLD STILL, KEEP QUIET AND WATCH ME...
TH DDD
sl ap
SHE *IS* VERY POWERFUL. SHE MANAGED TO DEFEAT ALL THOSE CRAB-RAWLER WITH A SINGLE MUDSDALE.
...
fw ump
rstl rstl

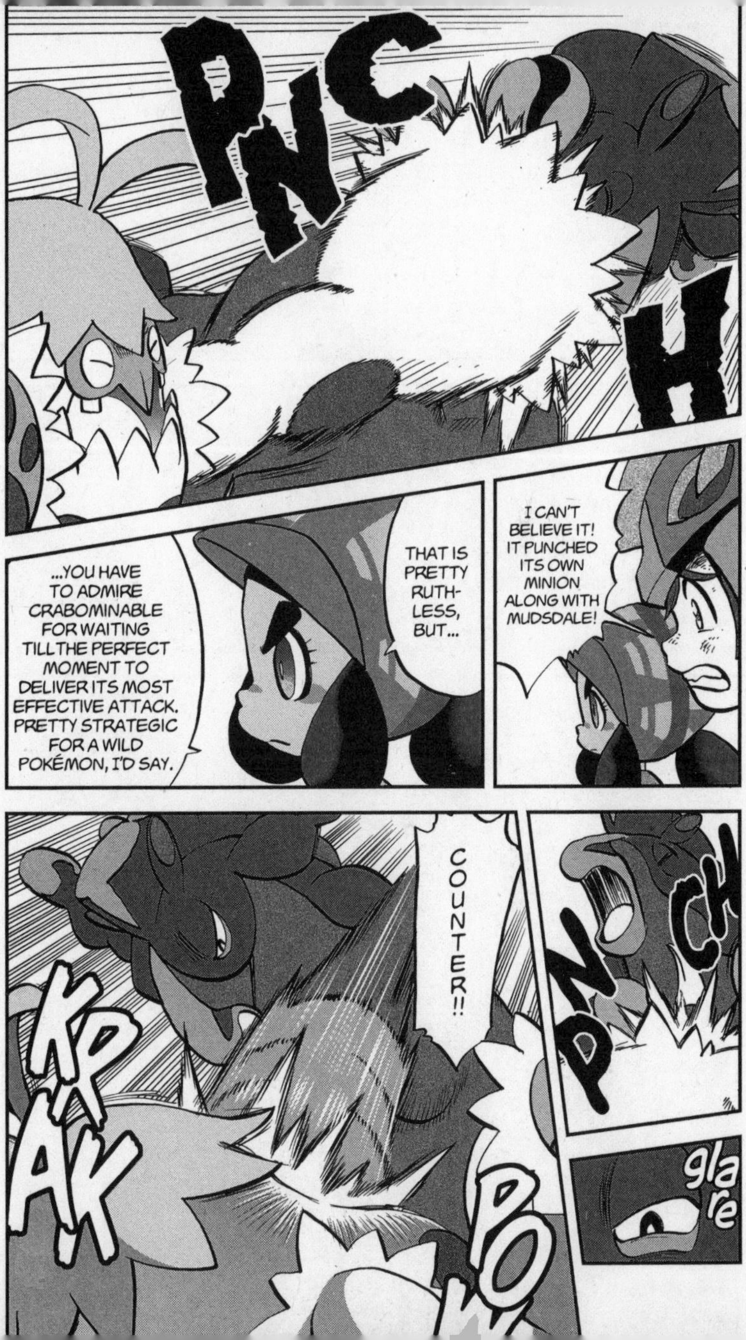
PNC
H
I CAN'T BELIEVE IT! IT PUNCHED ITS OWN MINION ALONG WITH MUDSDALE!
THAT IS PRETTY RUTH-LESS, BUT...
...YOU HAVE TO ADMIRE CRABOMINABLE FOR WAITING TILL THE PERFECT MOMENT TO DELIVER ITS MOST EFFECTIVE ATTACK. PRETTY STRATEGIC FOR A WILD POKÉMON, I'D SAY.
PNCH
glare
COUNTER!!
KRAK
BOOM

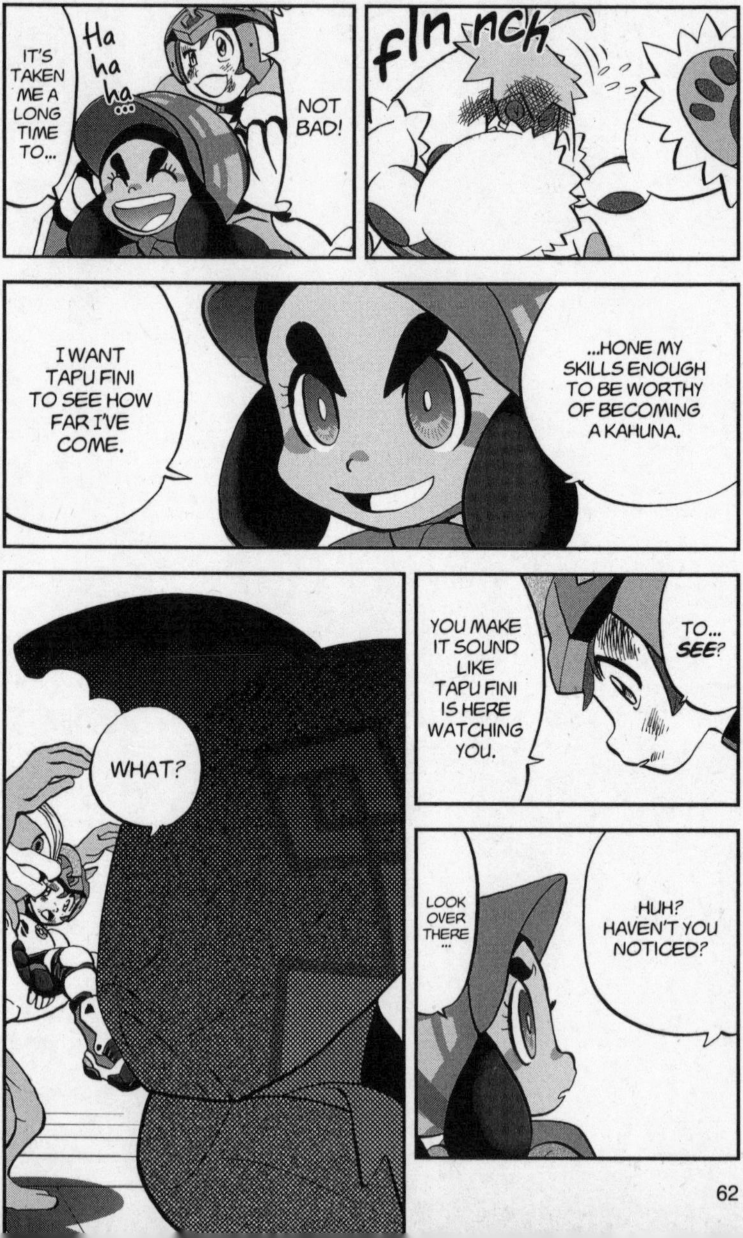
flinch
NOT BAD!
Ha ha ha...
IT'S TAKEN ME A LONG TIME TO...
...HONE MY SKILLS ENOUGH TO BE WORTHY OF BECOMING A KAHUNA.
I WANT TAPU FINI TO SEE HOW FAR I'VE COME.
TO... SEE?
YOU MAKE IT SOUND LIKE TAPU FINI IS HERE WATCHING YOU.
HUH? HAVEN'T YOU NOTICED?
LOOK OVER THERE...
WHAT?

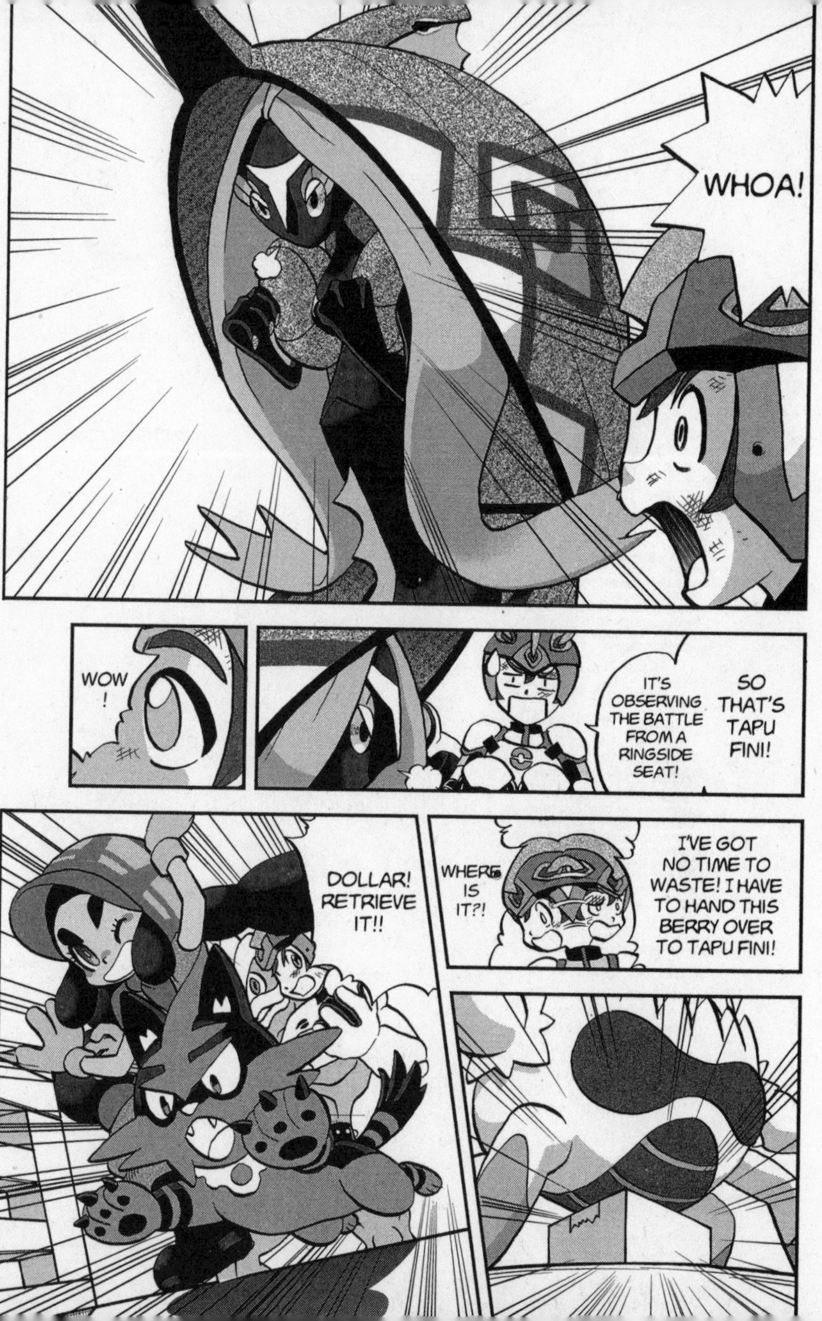
WHOA!
SO THAT'S TAPU FINI!
IT'S OBSERVING THE BATTLE FROM A RINGSIDE SEAT!
WOW!
I'VE GOT NO TIME TO WASTE! I HAVE TO HAND THIS BERRY OVER TO TAPU FINI!
WHERE IS IT?!
DOLLAR! RETRIEVE IT!!

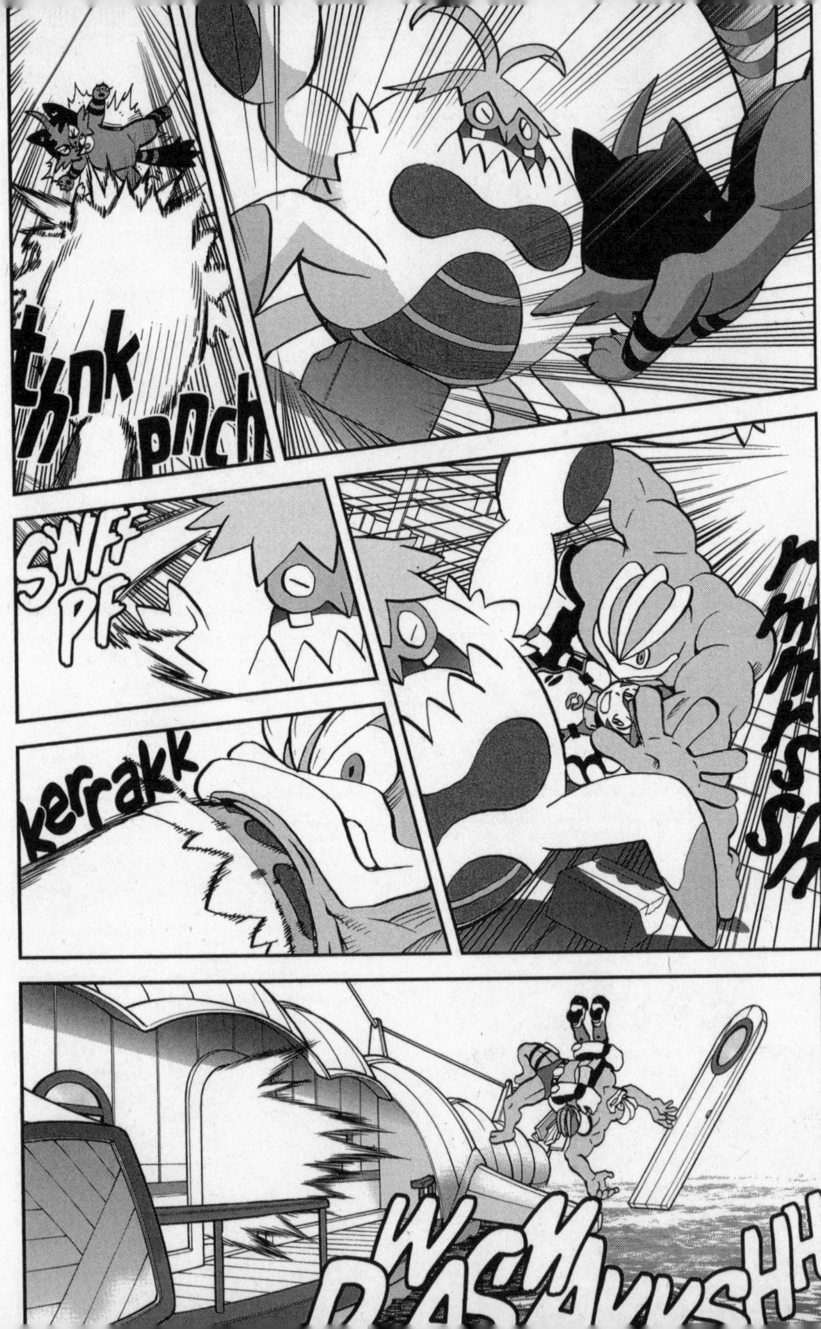
thnk pnch
SNFF PF
kerrakk

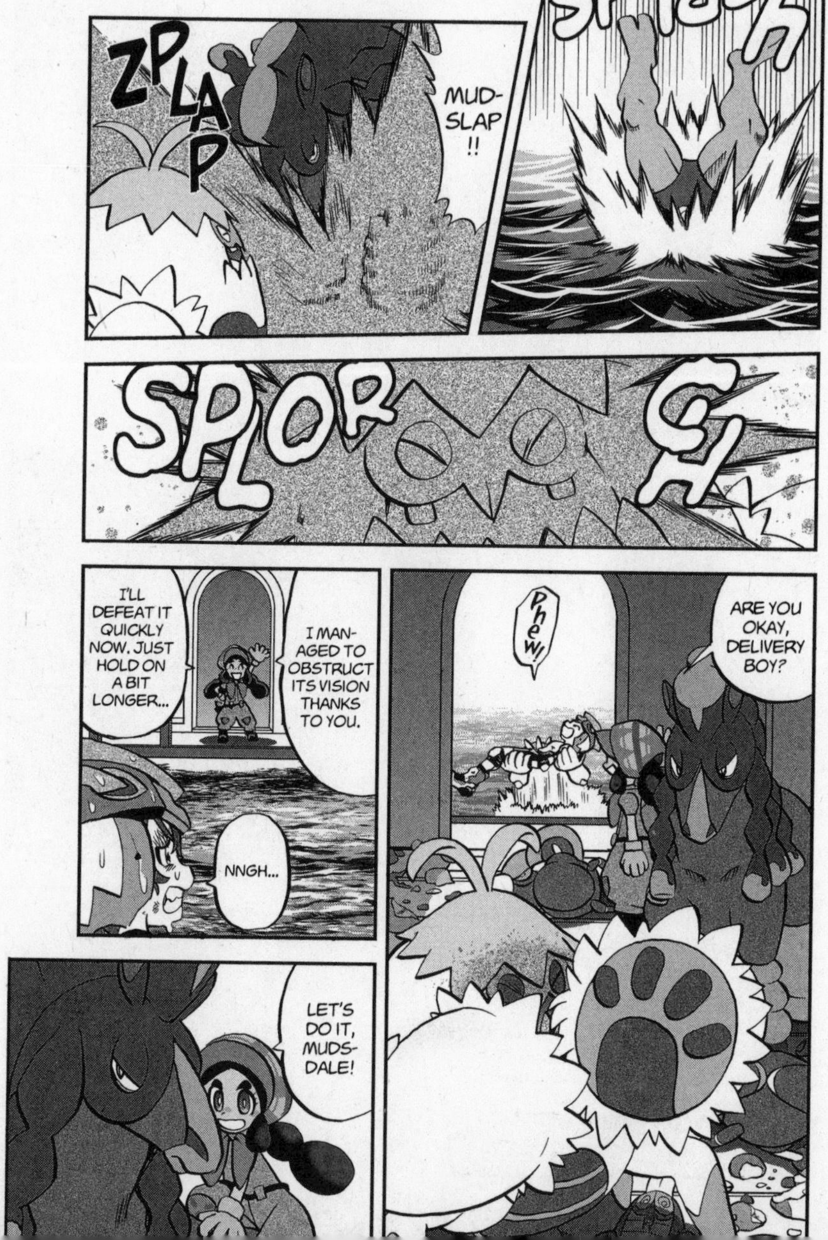
SPLASH
ZPLAP
MUD-SLAP !!
SPLORCH
ARE YOU OKAY, DELIVERY BOY?
Phew!!
I MAN-AGED TO OBSTRUCT ITS VISION THANKS TO YOU.
I'LL DEFEAT IT QUICKLY NOW. JUST HOLD ON A BIT LONGER...
NNGH...
LET'S DO IT, MUDS-DALE!

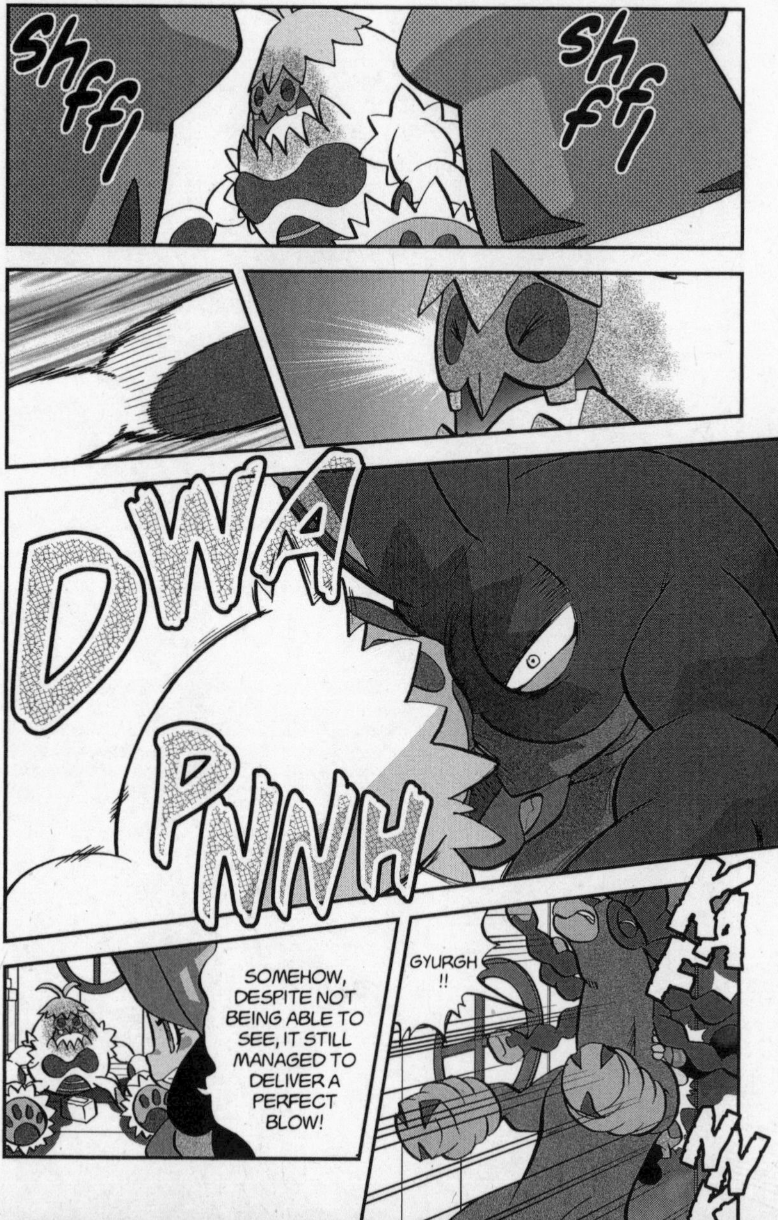
shffl
shffl
DWA
PNNH
GYURGH !!
KAF
NNK
SOMEHOW, DESPITE NOT BEING ABLE TO SEE, IT STILL MANAGED TO DELIVER A PERFECT BLOW!

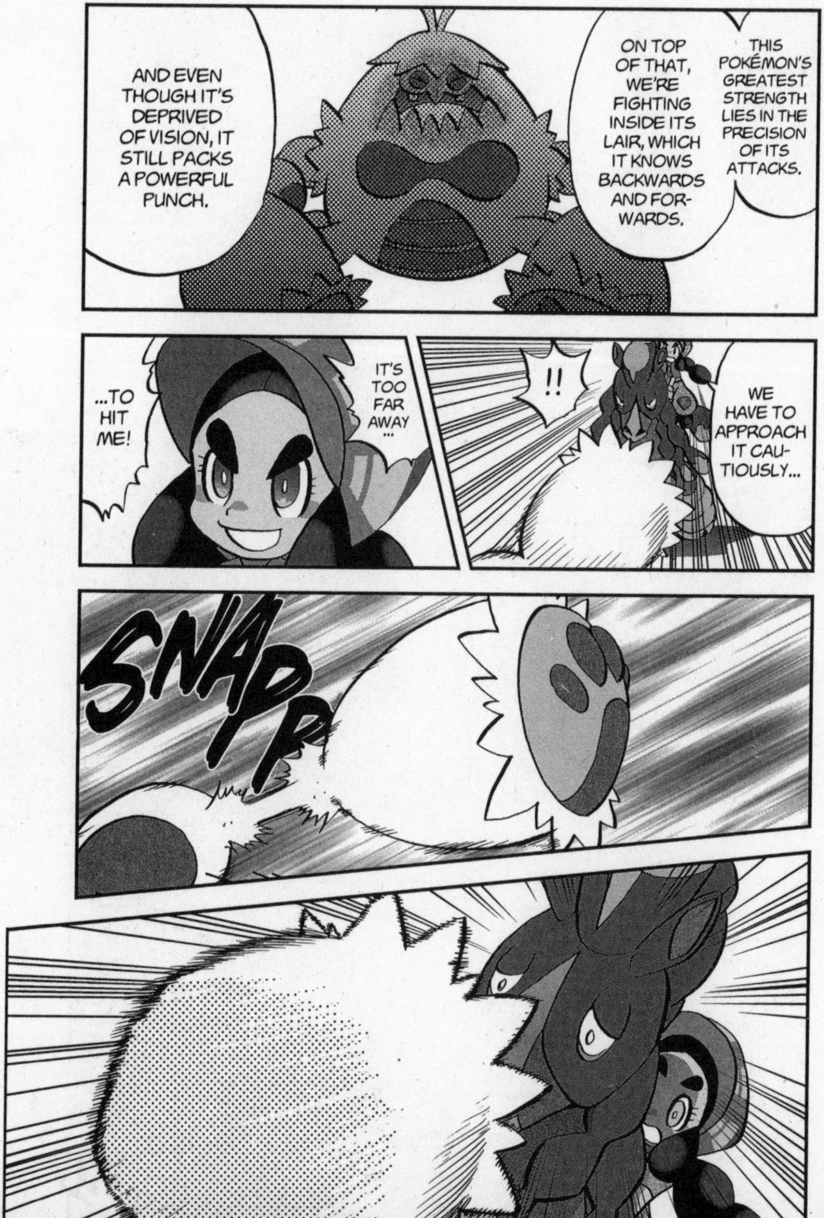
THIS POKÉMON'S GREATEST STRENGTH LIES IN THE PRECISION OF ITS ATTACKS.
ON TOP OF THAT, WE'RE FIGHTING INSIDE ITS LAIR, WHICH IT KNOWS BACKWARDS AND FOR-WARDS.
AND EVEN THOUGH IT'S DEPRIVED OF VISION, IT STILL PACKS A POWERFUL PUNCH.
WE HAVE TO APPROACH IT CAU-TIOUSLY...
!!
IT'S TOO FAR AWAY...
...TO HIT ME!
SNAP

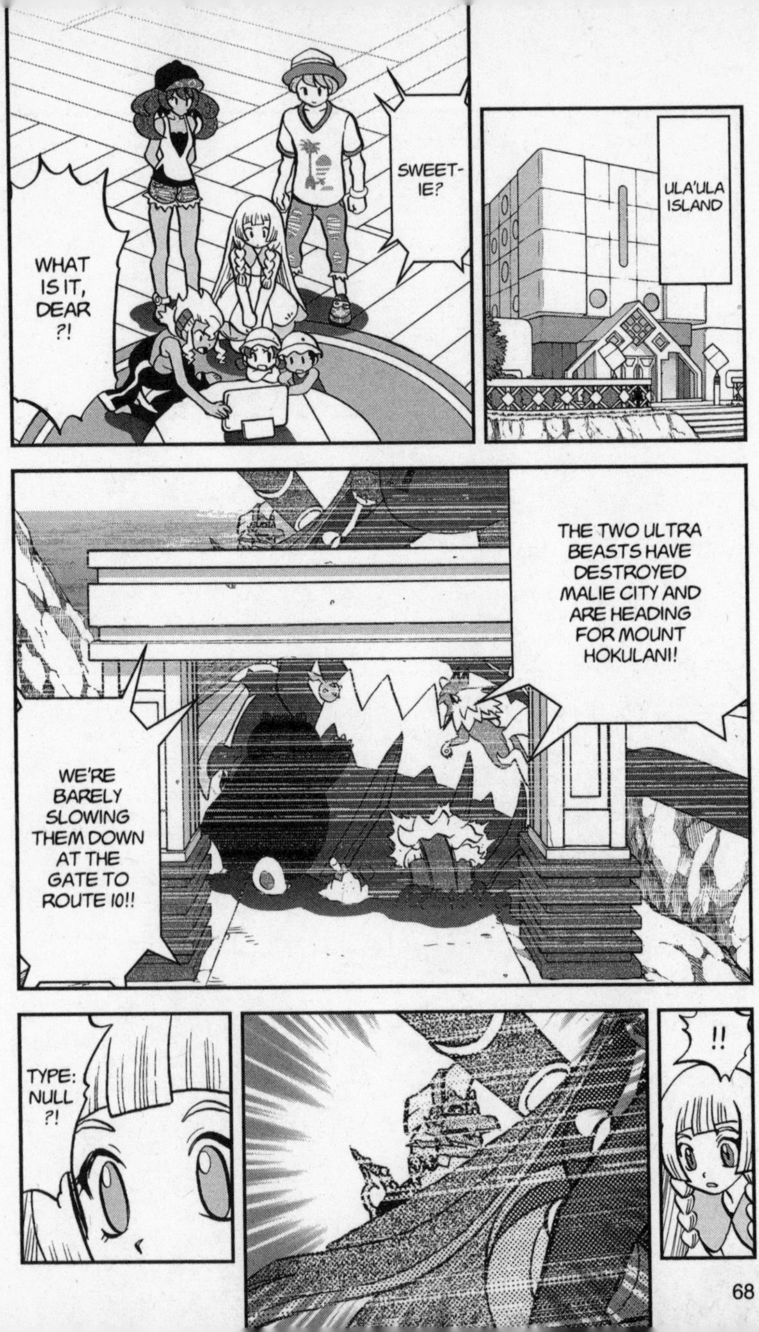
ULA'ULA ISLAND
SWEET-IE?
WHAT IS IT, DEAR?!
THE TWO ULTRA BEASTS HAVE DESTROYED MALIE CITY AND ARE HEADING FOR MOUNT HOKULANI!
WE'RE BARELY SLOWING THEM DOWN AT THE GATE TO ROUTE 10!!
!!
TYPE: NULL?!

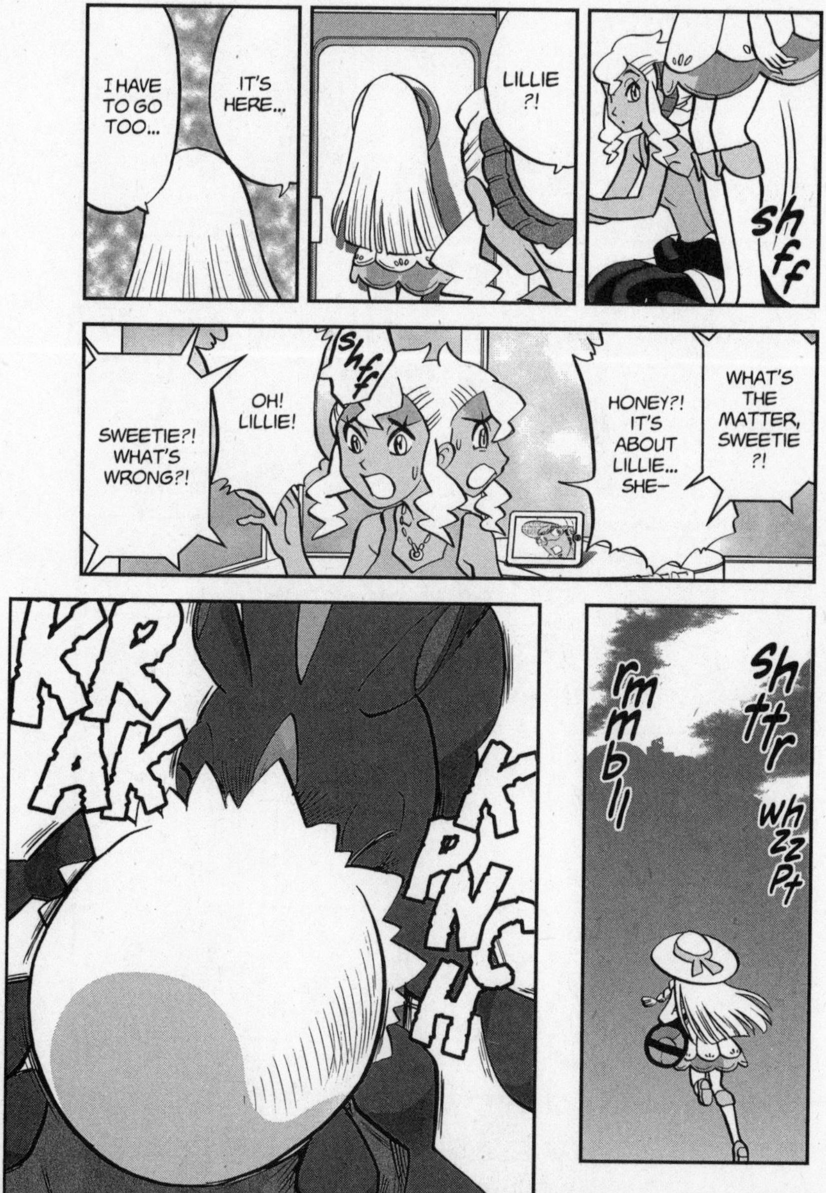
shff
LILLIE ?!
IT'S HERE...
I HAVE TO GO TOO...
WHAT'S THE MATTER, SWEETIE ?!
HONEY?! IT'S ABOUT LILLIE... SHE–
shff
OH! LILLIE!
SWEETIE?! WHAT'S WRONG?!
shttr
whzzpt
rmmbll
KPNCH
KRAK

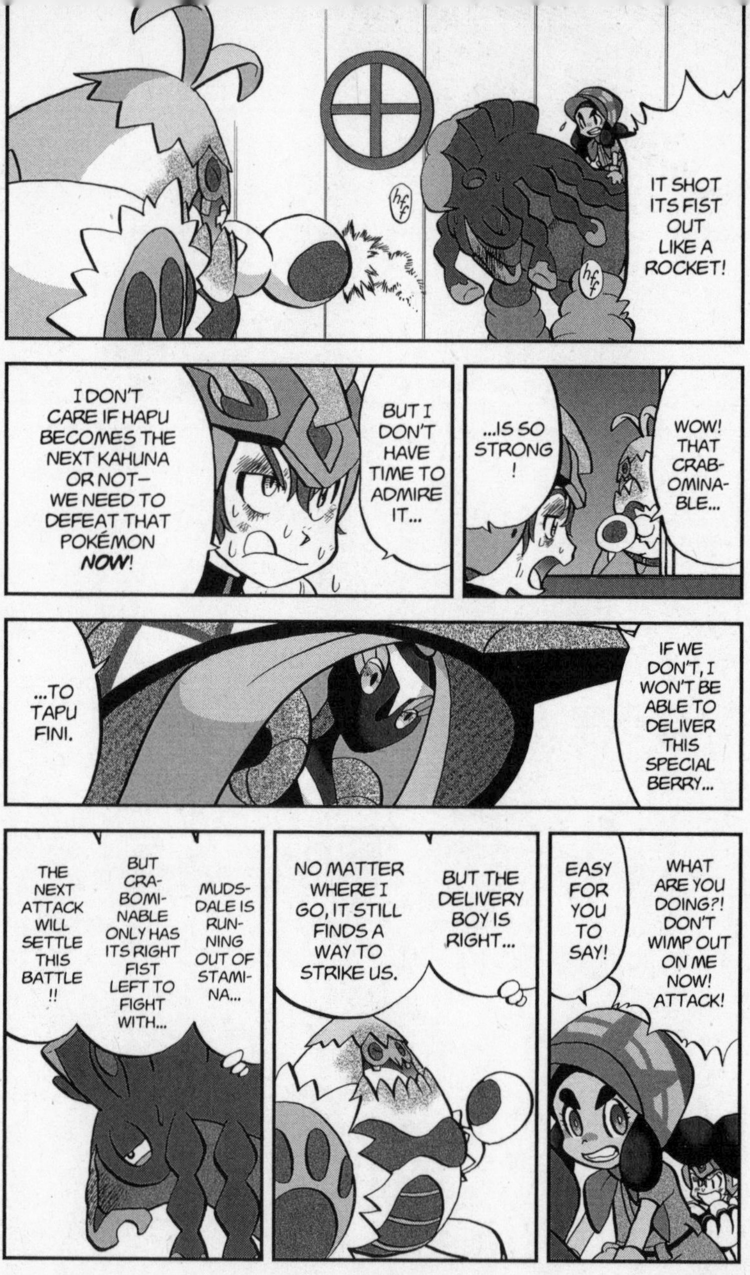
IT SHOT ITS FIST OUT LIKE A ROCKET!
hff
hff
WOW! THAT CRAB-OMINA-BLE...
...IS SO STRONG!
BUT I DON'T HAVE TIME TO ADMIRE IT...
I DON'T CARE IF HAPU BECOMES THE NEXT KAHUNA OR NOT— WE NEED TO DEFEAT THAT POKÉMON NOW!
IF WE DON'T, I WON'T BE ABLE TO DELIVER THIS SPECIAL BERRY...
...TO TAPU FINI.
WHAT ARE YOU DOING?! DON'T WIMP OUT ON ME NOW! ATTACK!
EASY FOR YOU TO SAY!
BUT THE DELIVERY BOY IS RIGHT...
NO MATTER WHERE I GO, IT STILL FINDS A WAY TO STRIKE US.
MUDS-DALE IS RUN-NING OUT OF STAMI-NA...
BUT CRA-BOMI-NABLE ONLY HAS ITS RIGHT FIST LEFT TO FIGHT WITH...
THE NEXT ATTACK WILL SETTLE THIS BATTLE!!

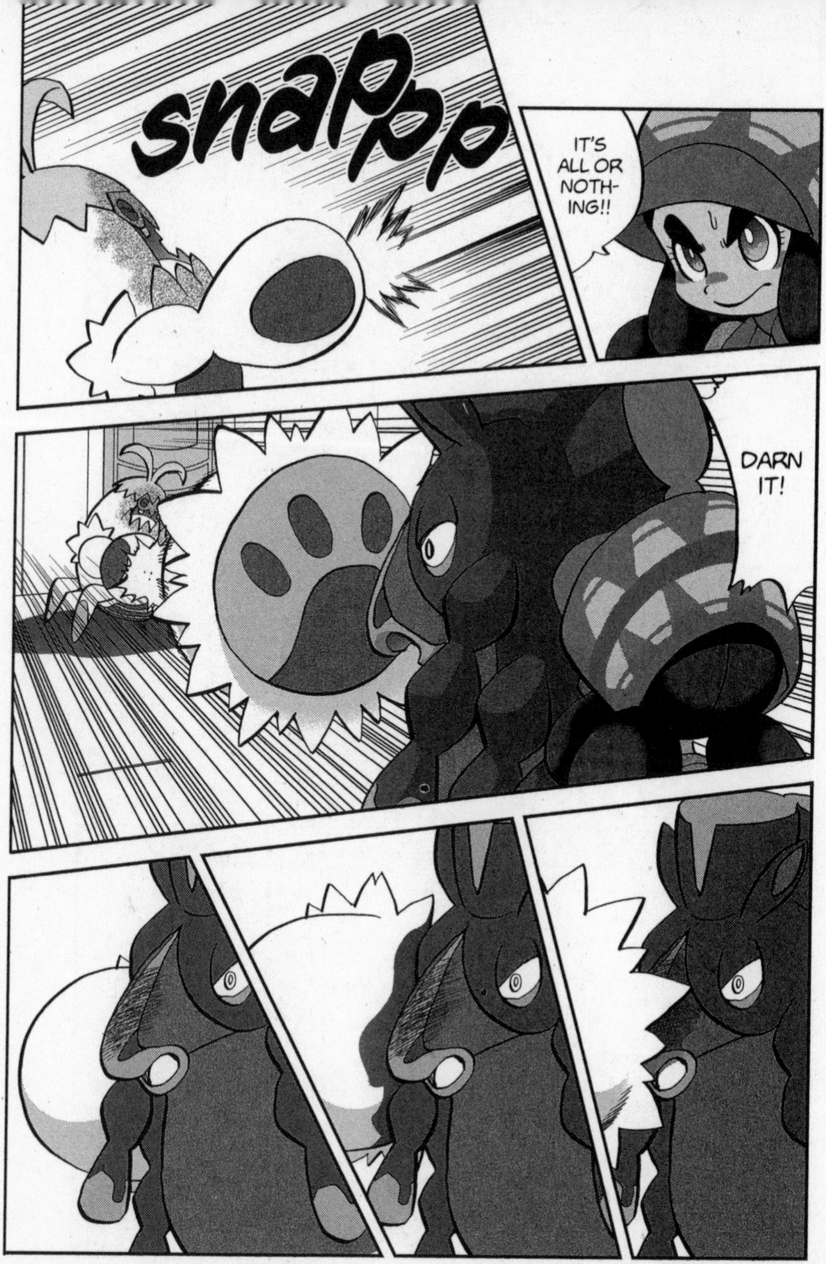
IT'S ALL OR NOTH-ING!!
snappp
DARN IT!

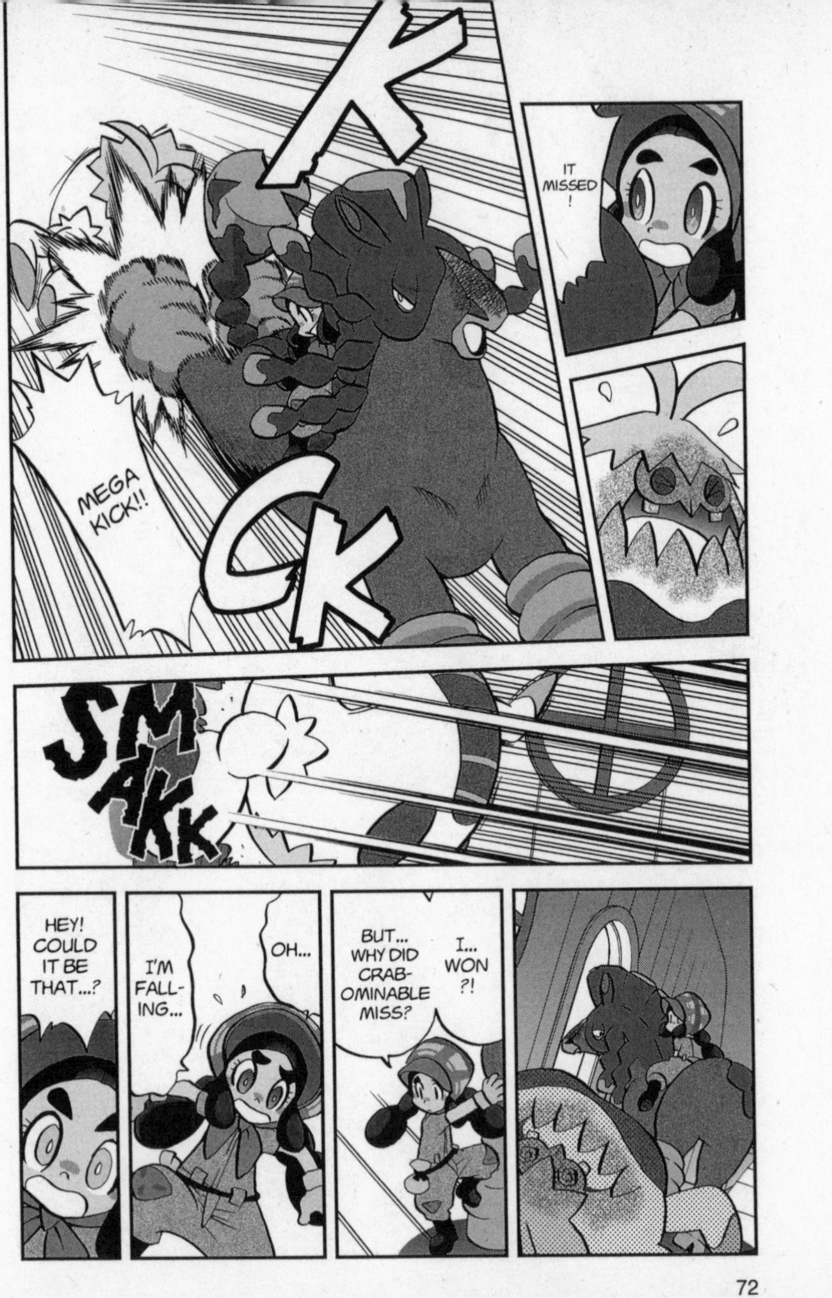
IT MISSED!
MEGA KICK!!
SMAKK
I... WON?!
BUT... WHY DID CRAB-OMINABLE MISS?
OH...
I'M FALLING...
HEY! COULD IT BE THAT...?

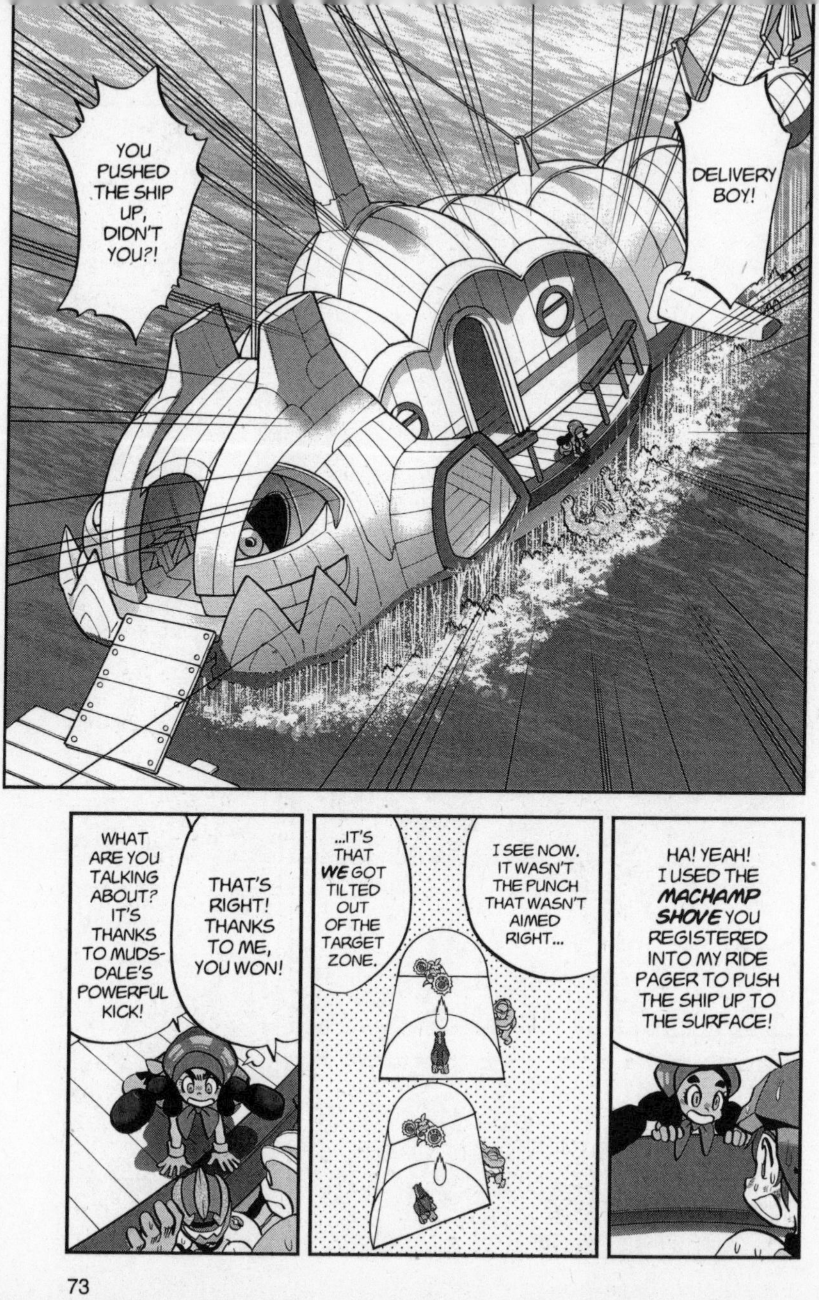
DELIVERY BOY!
YOU PUSHED THE SHIP UP, DIDN'T YOU?!
HA! YEAH! I USED THE ***MACHAMP SHOVE*** YOU REGISTERED INTO MY RIDE PAGER TO PUSH THE SHIP UP TO THE SURFACE!
I SEE NOW. IT WASN'T THE PUNCH THAT WASN'T AIMED RIGHT...
...IT'S THAT ***WE*** GOT TILTED OUT OF THE TARGET ZONE.
THAT'S RIGHT! THANKS TO ME, YOU WON!
WHAT ARE YOU TALKING ABOUT? IT'S THANKS TO MUDS-DALE'S POWERFUL KICK!

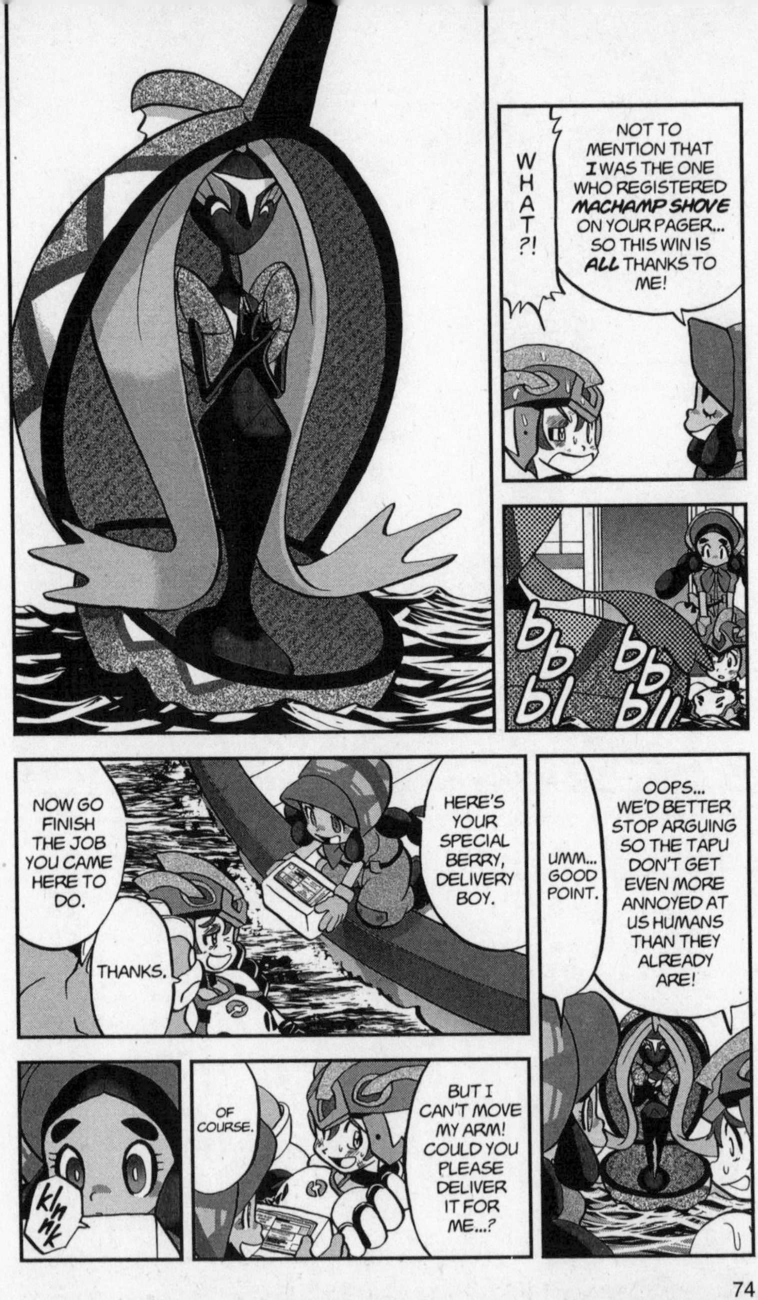
NOT TO MENTION THAT I WAS THE ONE WHO REGISTERED MACHAMP SHOVE ON YOUR PAGER... SO THIS WIN IS ALL THANKS TO ME!
WHAT?!
bbbl
bbbll
OOPS... WE'D BETTER STOP ARGUING SO THE TAPU DON'T GET EVEN MORE ANNOYED AT US HUMANS THAN THEY ALREADY ARE!
UMM... GOOD POINT.
HERE'S YOUR SPECIAL BERRY, DELIVERY BOY.
NOW GO FINISH THE JOB YOU CAME HERE TO DO.
THANKS.
BUT I CAN'T MOVE MY ARM! COULD YOU PLEASE DELIVER IT FOR ME...?
OF COURSE.
klnk

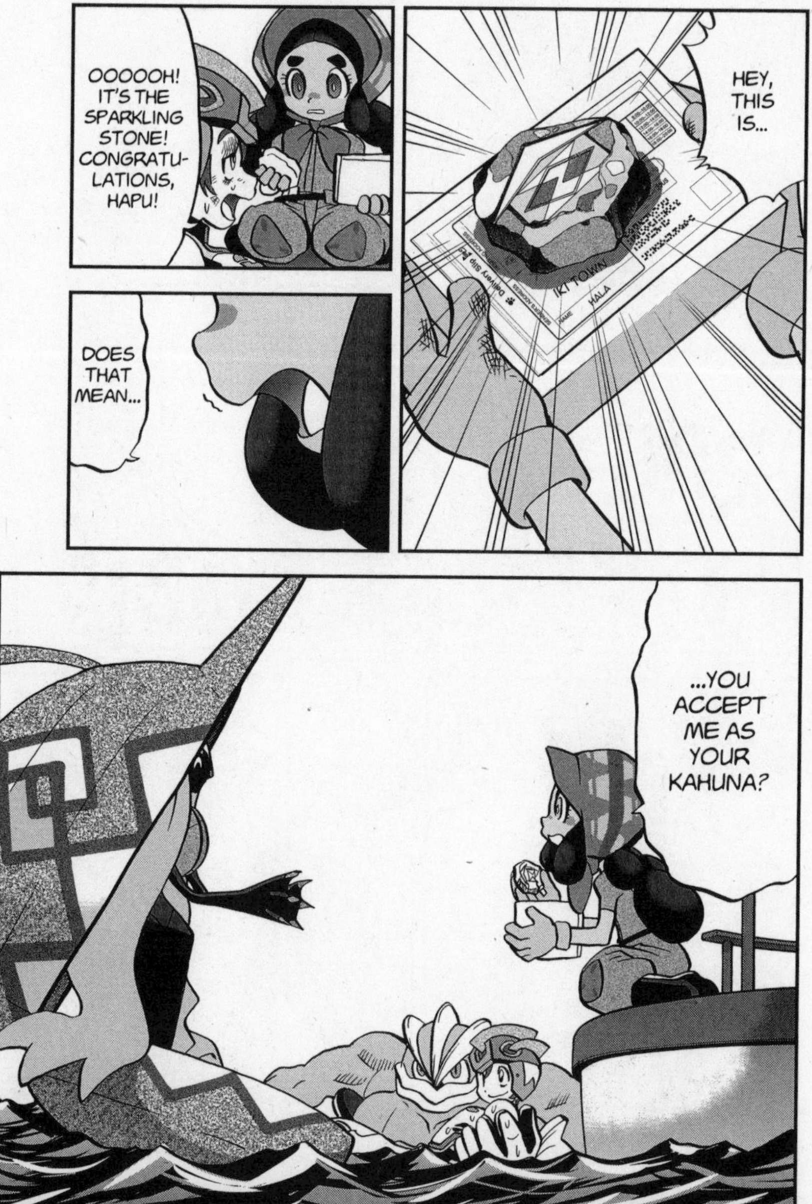
HEY, THIS IS...
IKI TOWN
HALA
OOOOOH! IT'S THE SPARKLING STONE! CONGRATULATIONS, HAPU!
DOES THAT MEAN...
...YOU ACCEPT ME AS YOUR KAHUNA?

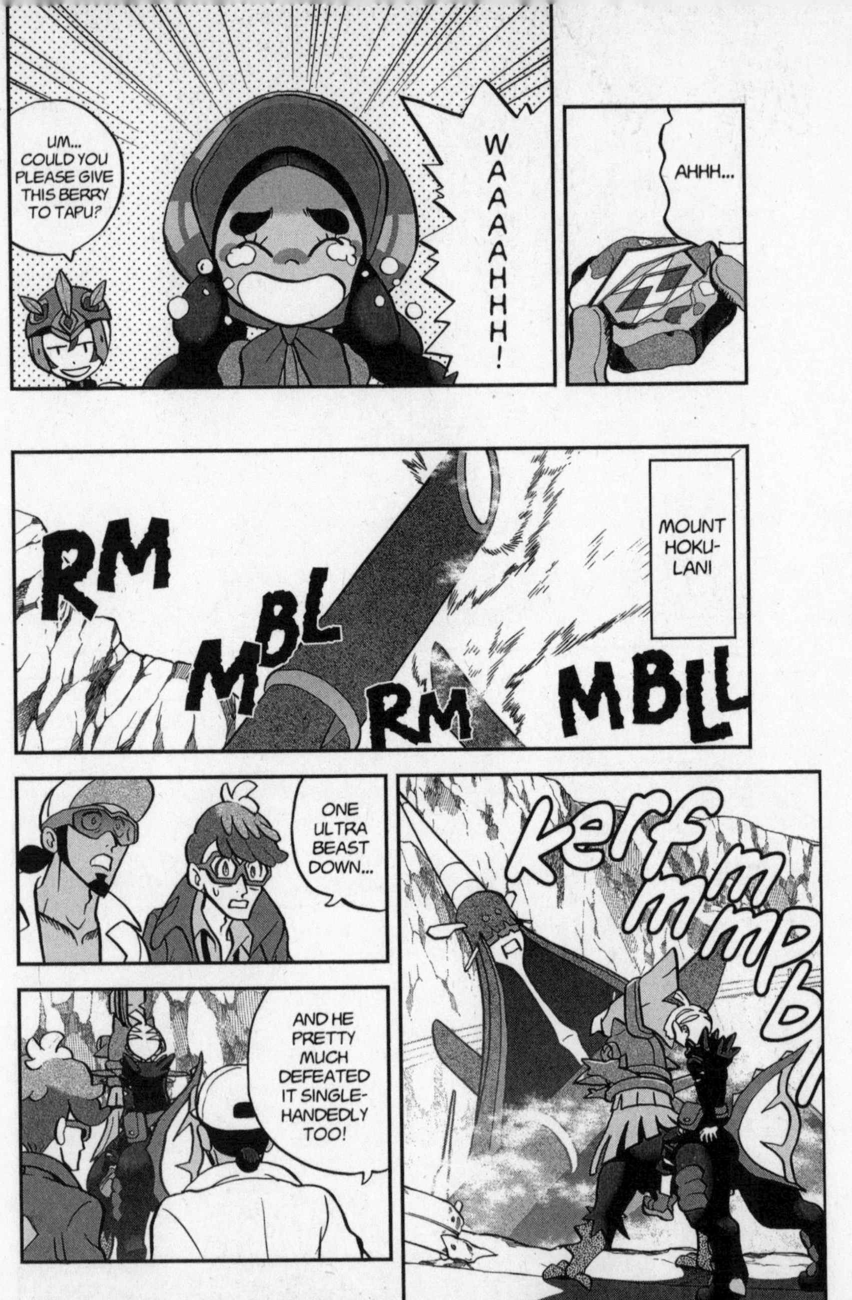
AHHH...
WAAAAAHHH!
UM... COULD YOU PLEASE GIVE THIS BERRY TO TAPU?
MOUNT HOKU-LANI
RMMBL
RMMBLL
kerfmmmpb
ONE ULTRA BEAST DOWN...
AND HE PRETTY MUCH DEFEATED IT SINGLE-HANDEDLY TOO!

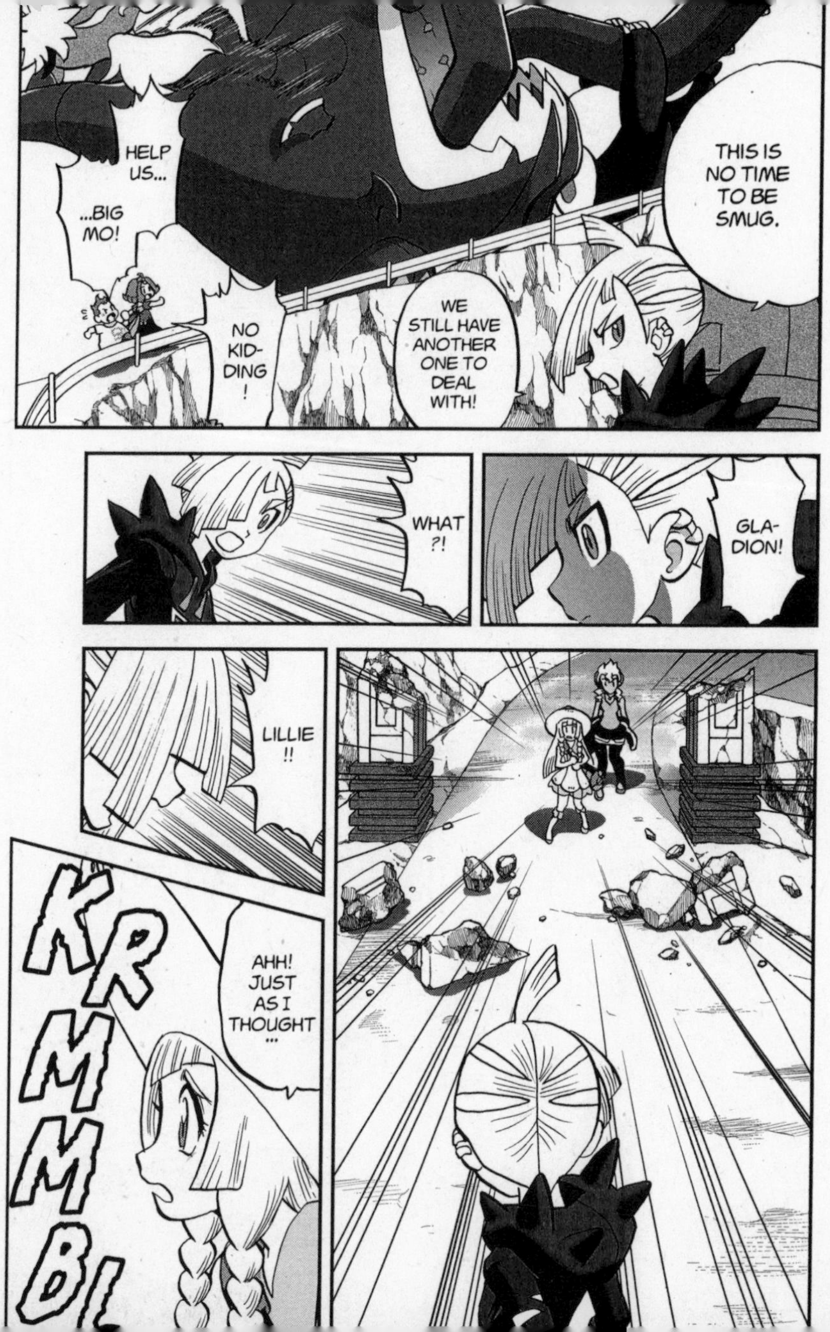
THIS IS NO TIME TO BE SMUG.
WE STILL HAVE ANOTHER ONE TO DEAL WITH!
NO KIDDING!
HELP US...
...BIG MO!
GLADION!
WHAT?!
LILLIE!!
KRMMMBL
AHH! JUST AS I THOUGHT...

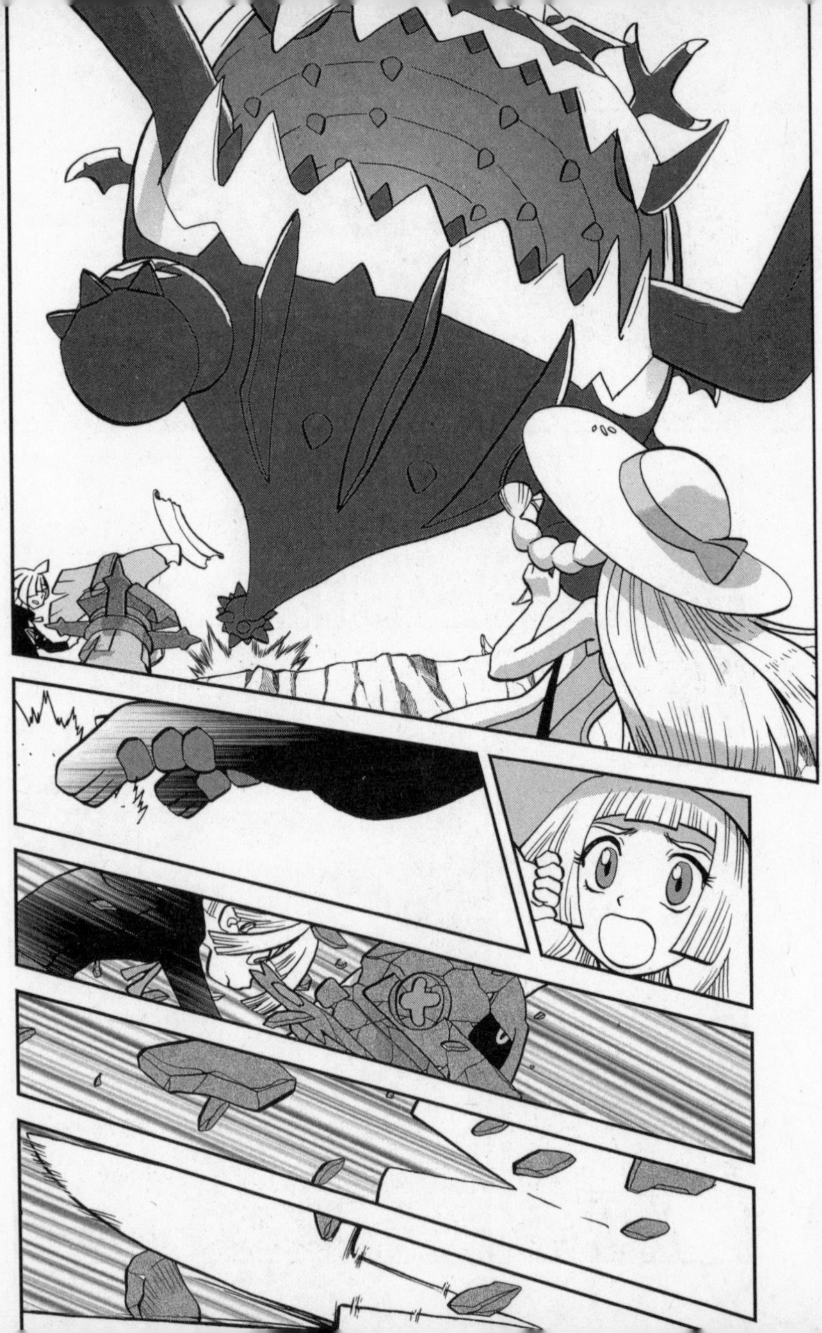

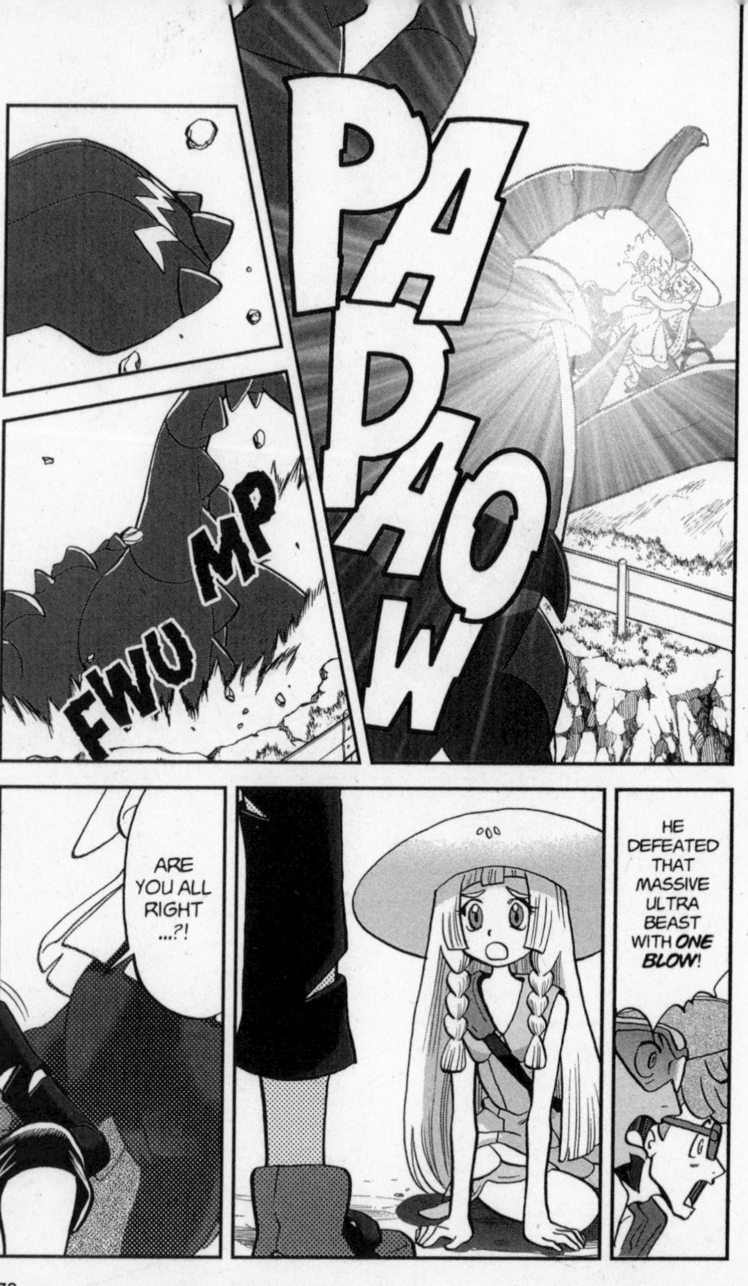
PADAPAOW
FWUMP
HE DEFEATED THAT MASSIVE ULTRA BEAST WITH ONE BLOW!
ARE YOU ALL RIGHT ...?!

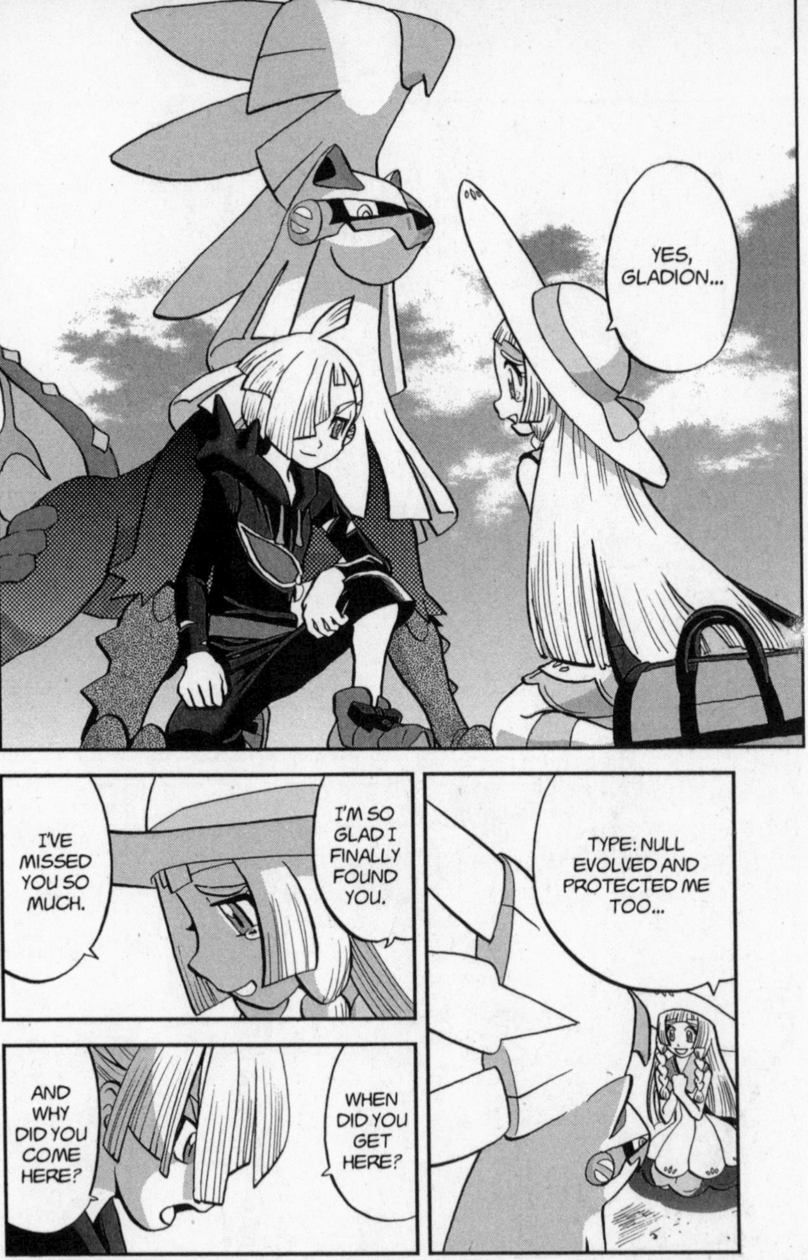
YES, GLADION...
TYPE: NULL EVOLVED AND PROTECTED ME TOO...
I'M SO GLAD I FINALLY FOUND YOU.
I'VE MISSED YOU SO MUCH.
WHEN DID YOU GET HERE?
AND WHY DID YOU COME HERE?

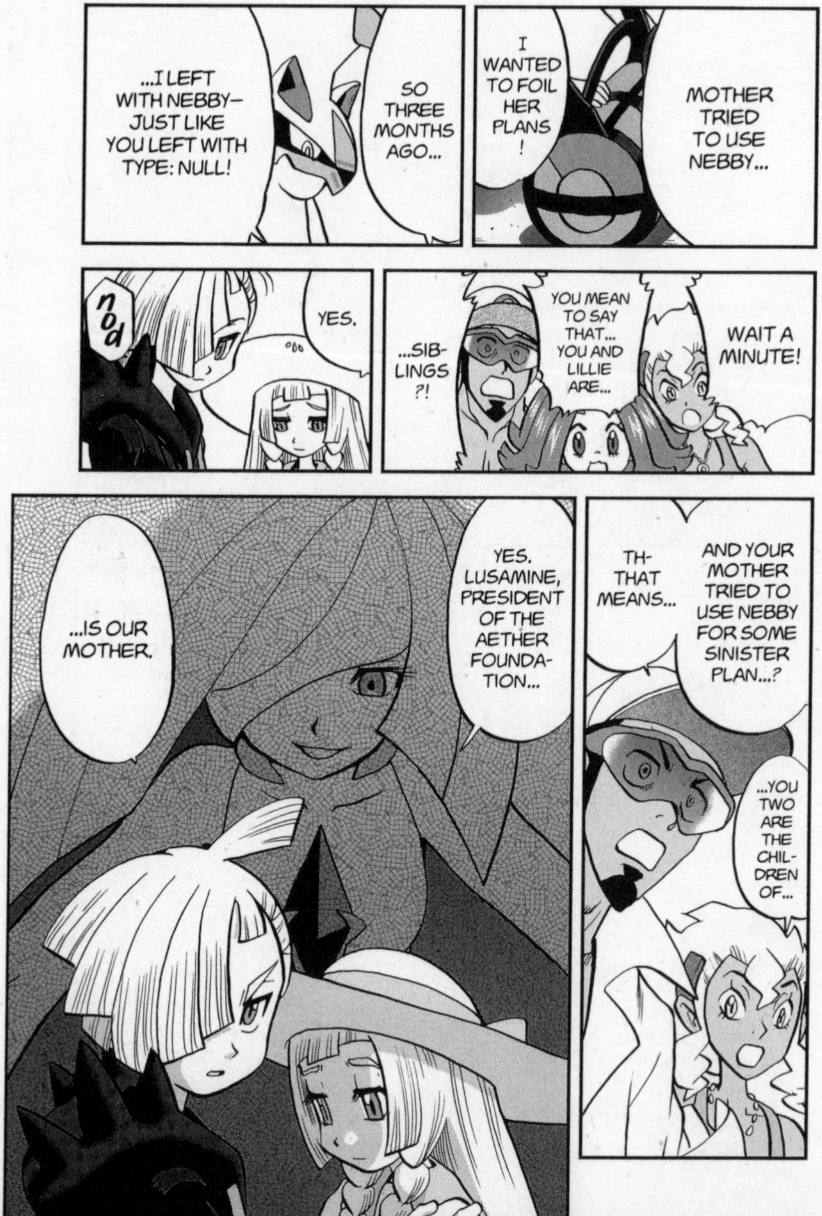
MOTHER TRIED TO USE NEBBY...
I WANTED TO FOIL HER PLANS!
SO THREE MONTHS AGO...
...I LEFT WITH NEBBY—JUST LIKE YOU LEFT WITH TYPE: NULL!
WAIT A MINUTE!
YOU MEAN TO SAY THAT... YOU AND LILLIE ARE...
...SIB-LINGS?!
YES.
nod
AND YOUR MOTHER TRIED TO USE NEBBY FOR SOME SINISTER PLAN...?
TH-THAT MEANS...
...YOU TWO ARE THE CHIL-DREN OF...
YES. LUSAMINE, PRESIDENT OF THE AETHER FOUNDATION...
...IS OUR MOTHER.

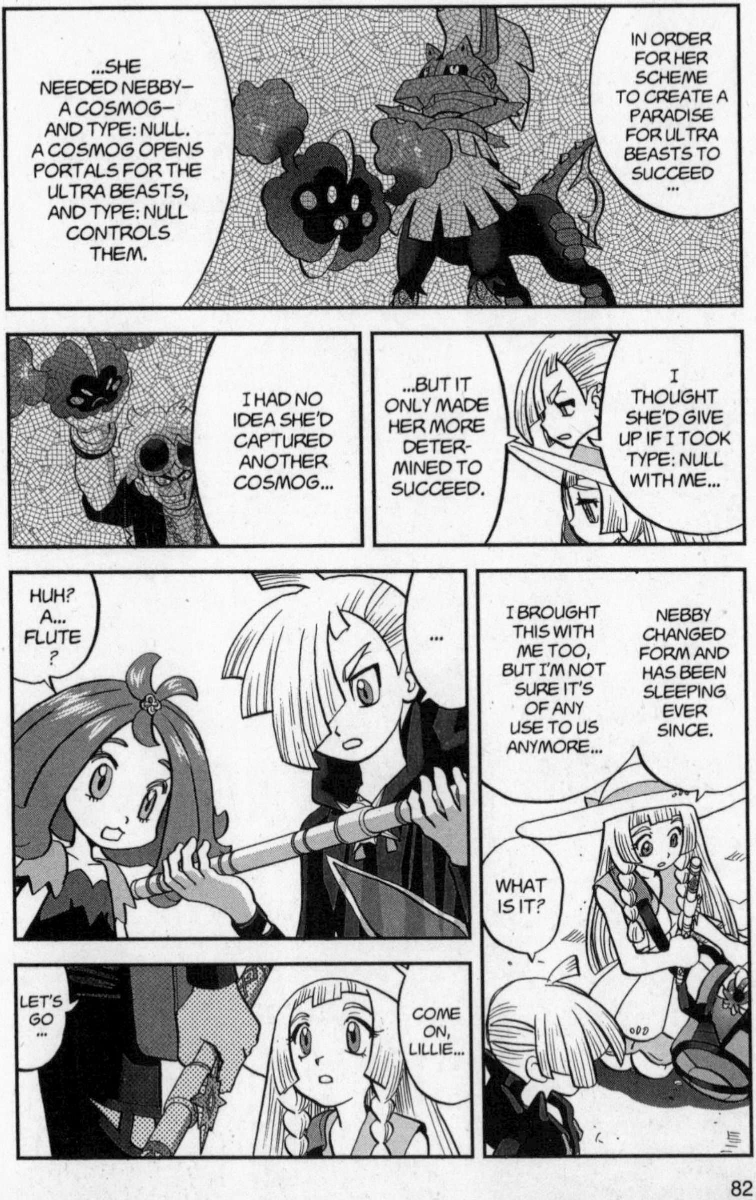
IN ORDER FOR HER SCHEME TO CREATE A PARADISE FOR ULTRA BEASTS TO SUCCEED...
...SHE NEEDED NEBBY—A COSMOG—AND TYPE: NULL. A COSMOG OPENS PORTALS FOR THE ULTRA BEASTS, AND TYPE: NULL CONTROLS THEM.
I THOUGHT SHE'D GIVE UP IF I TOOK TYPE: NULL WITH ME...
...BUT IT ONLY MADE HER MORE DETER-MINED TO SUCCEED.
I HAD NO IDEA SHE'D CAPTURED ANOTHER COSMOG...
NEBBY CHANGED FORM AND HAS BEEN SLEEPING EVER SINCE.
I BROUGHT THIS WITH ME TOO, BUT I'M NOT SURE IT'S OF ANY USE TO US ANYMORE...
WHAT IS IT?
...
HUH? A... FLUTE?
COME ON, LILLIE...
LET'S GO...

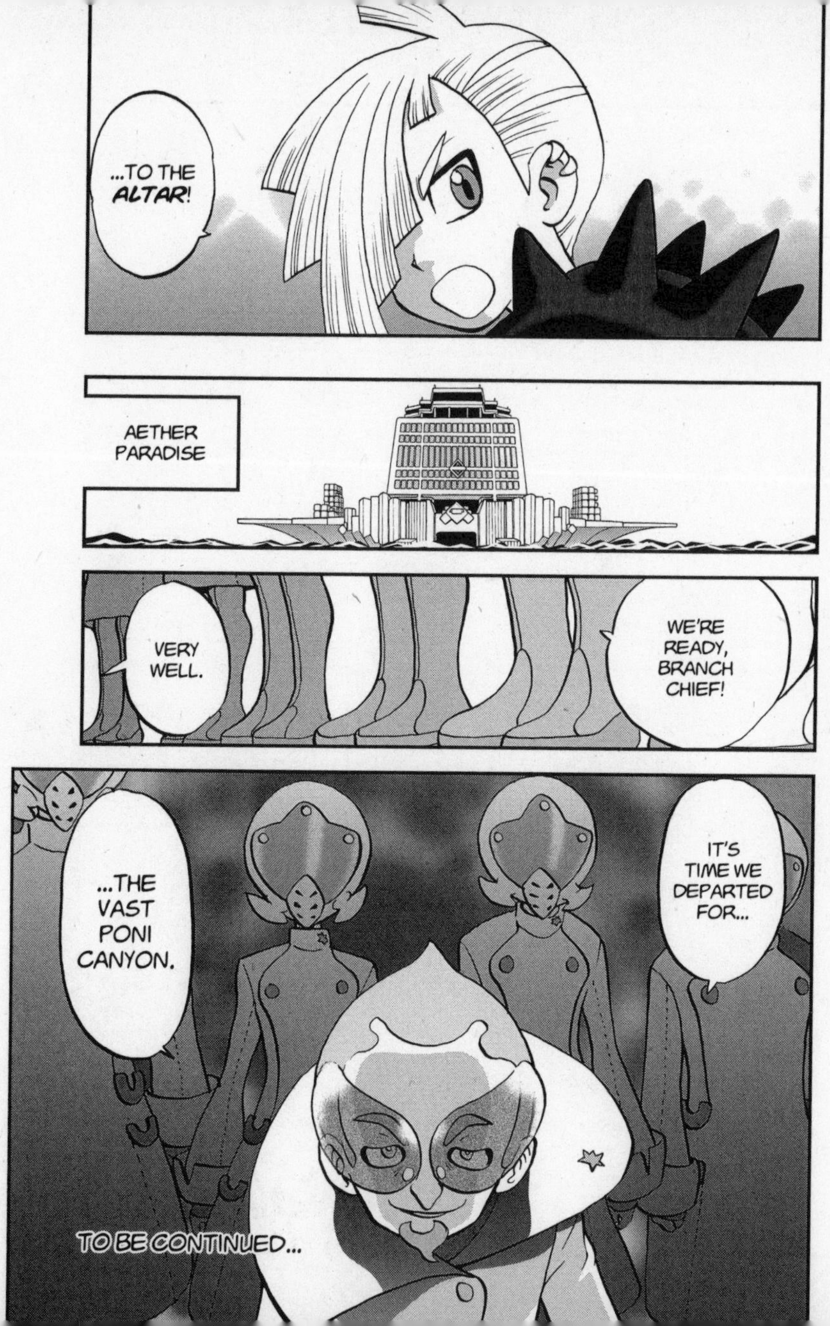
...TO THE ALTAR!
AETHER PARADISE
WE'RE READY, BRANCH CHIEF!
VERY WELL.
IT'S TIME WE DEPARTED FOR...
...THE VAST PONI CANYON.
TO BE CONTINUED...

🌺 Cafe & Restaurant

ALOLA! PLEASURE TO MEET YOU!

HELLO, PROFESSOR BURNET. I'M MOON.

Food and beverages can be ordered at the Pokémon Center Cafe. If you're tired from battling, take a break over a nice cup of Tapu Cocoa. Relax and enjoy yourself.

Mallow's restaurant is popular too! ♪

Guide to Alola 19

**Pokémon Sun & Moon
Volume 7
VIZ Media Edition**

Story by HIDENORI KUSAKA
Art by SATOSHI YAMAMOTO

©2020 The Pokémon Company International.
©1995–2019 Nintendo / Creatures Inc. / GAME FREAK inc.
TM, ®, and character names are trademarks of Nintendo.
POCKET MONSTERS SPECIAL SUN • MOON Vol. 4
by Hidenori KUSAKA, Satoshi YAMAMOTO
© 2017 Hidenori KUSAKA, Satoshi YAMAMOTO
All rights reserved.
Original Japanese edition published by SHOGAKUKAN.
English translation rights in the United States of America, Canada, the United Kingdom,
Ireland, Australia and New Zealand arranged with SHOGAKUKAN.

Original Cover Design—Hiroyuki KAWASOME (grafio)

English Adaptation—Bryant Turnage
Translation—Tetsuichiro Miyaki
Touch-Up & Lettering—Susan Daigle-Leach
Design—Alice Lewis
Editor—Annette Roman

Printed in the U.S.A.

Published by
VIZ Media, LLC
P.O. Box 77010
San Francisco, CA 94107

10 9 8 7 6 5 4 3 2 1
First printing, May 2020

viz.com

Coming Next Volume

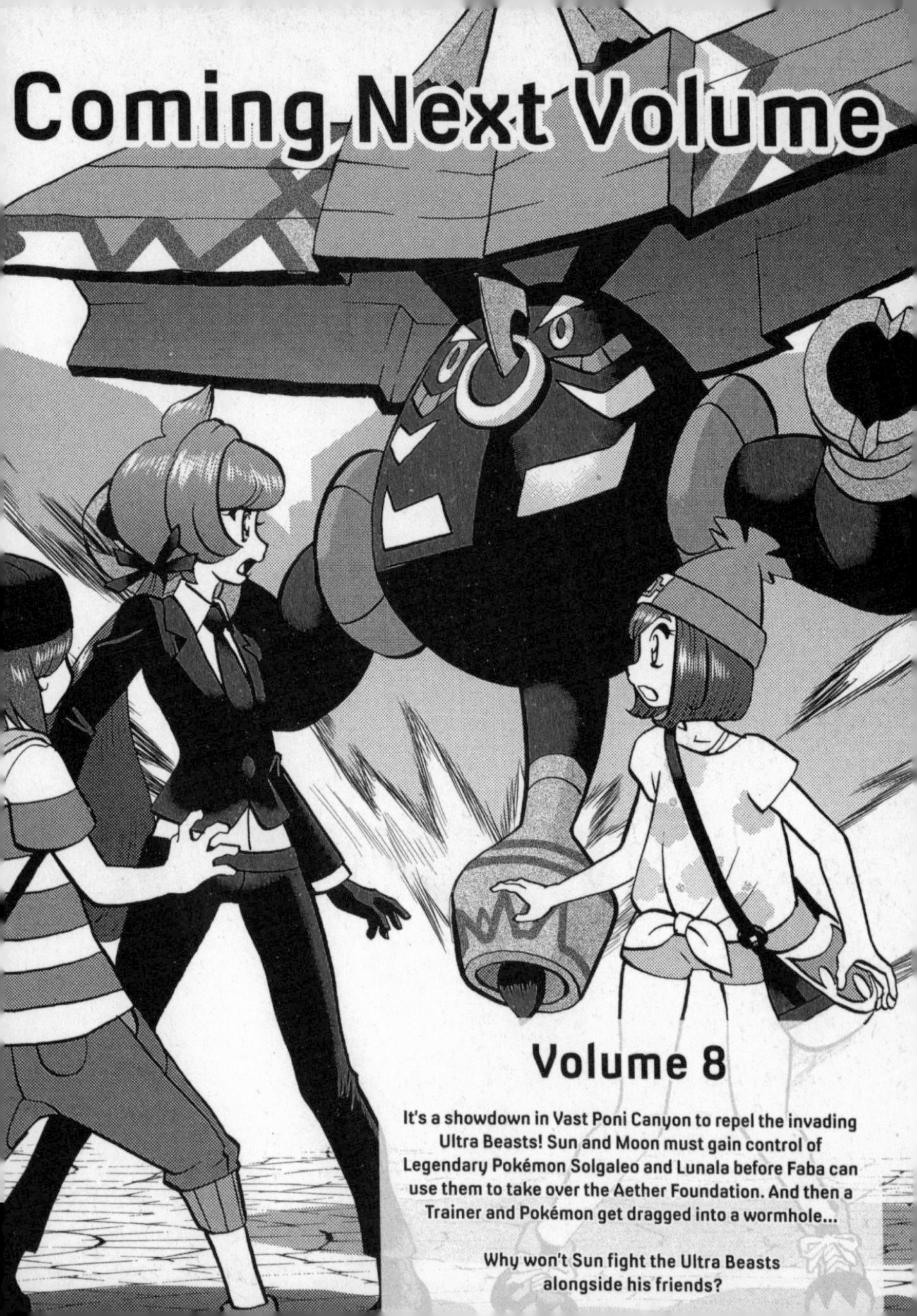

Volume 8

It's a showdown in Vast Poni Canyon to repel the invading Ultra Beasts! Sun and Moon must gain control of Legendary Pokémon Solgaleo and Lunala before Faba can use them to take over the Aether Foundation. And then a Trainer and Pokémon get dragged into a wormhole...

Why won't Sun fight the Ultra Beasts alongside his friends?

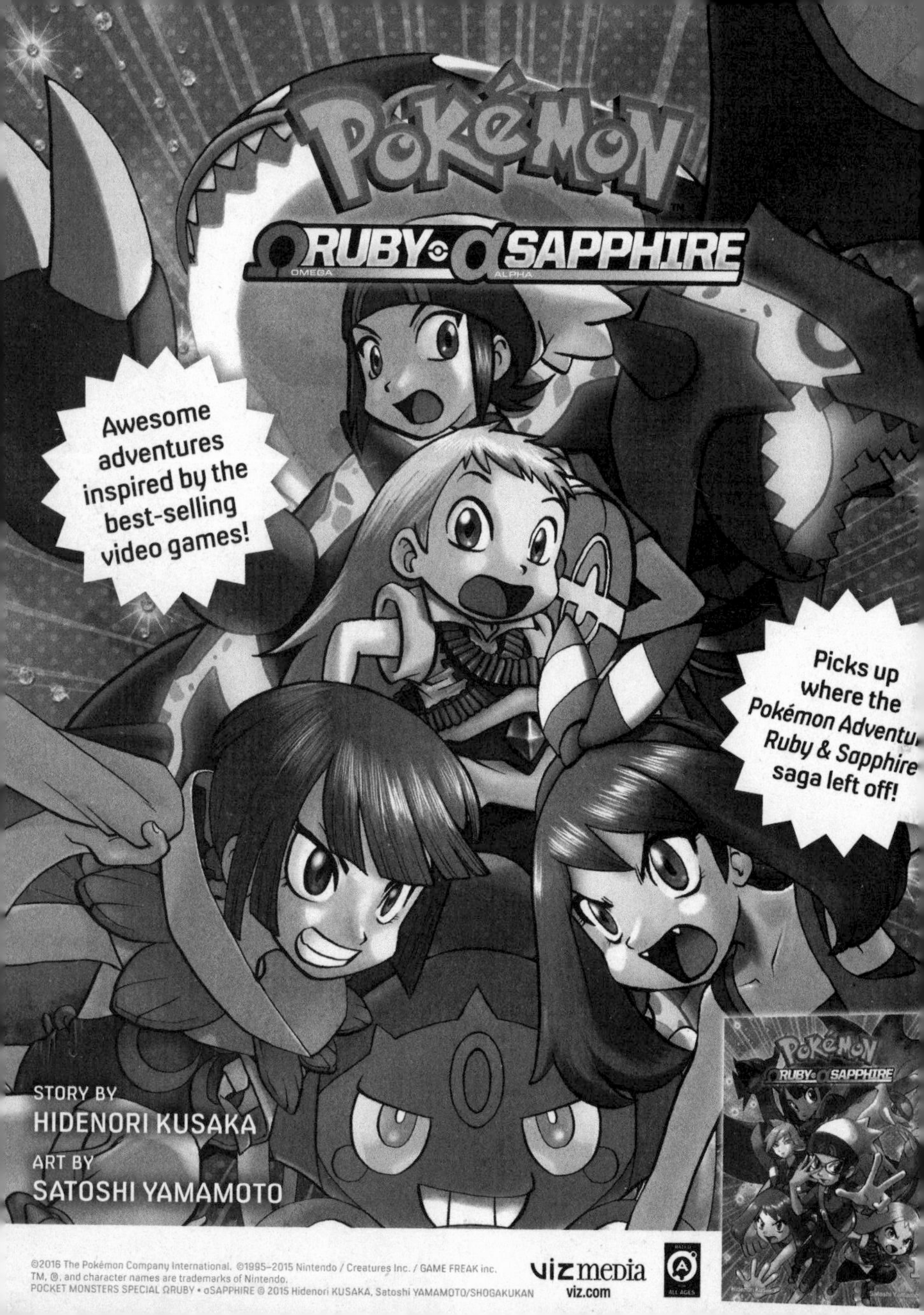

POKÉMON
ΩRUBY • αSAPPHIRE
OMEGA ALPHA
Awesome adventures inspired by the best-selling video games!
Picks up where the Pokémon Adventu Ruby & Sapphire saga left off!
STORY BY
HIDENORI KUSAKA
ART BY
SATOSHI YAMAMOTO

THIS IS THE END OF THIS GRAPHIC NOVEL!

To properly enjoy this VIZ Media graphic novel, pleas turn it around and begin reading from right to left.

This book has been printed in the original Japanese format in order to preserve the orientation of the original artwork. Have fun with it!

<<<< READ THIS WAY!

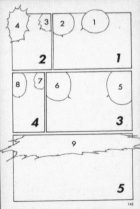

Follow the action this way.